# FELIX
## UNLIMITED

Books by Andrew Norriss

*Mike*
*Jessica's Ghost*
*Archie's Unbelievably Freaky Week*
*I Don't Believe It, Archie!*
*Aquila*
*Aquila 2*
*Ctrl-Z*
*The Portal*
*The Unluckiest Boy in the World*
*The Touchstone*
*Bernard's Watch*
*Matt's Million*
*Woof! Tales*

# FELIX
## UNLIMITED

### ANDREW NORRISS

**David Fickling Books**

31 Beaumont Street
Oxford OX1 2NP, UK

Felix Unlimited
is a
DAVID FICKLING BOOK

First published in Great Britain in 2021 by
David Fickling Books,
31 Beaumont Street,
Oxford, OX1 2NP

Text © Andrew Norriss, 2021
Cover and illustrations © Sarah Horne, 2021

978-1-78845-205-2

1 3 5 7 9 10 8 6 4 2

DAVID FICKLING BOOKS Reg. No. 8340307

A CIP catalogue record for this book is available from the British Library.

Typeset in 11/18 pt Sabon by Falcon Oast Graphic Art Ltd.
Printed and bound in Great Britain by Clays, Ltd., Elcograf S.p.A.

*For the real Anthony Coleman.*
*A most magical man.*

*The events in this story happened some years ago, at a time when the internet was new, and people were still working out what it could do.*

*Some of those people were remarkably young . . .*

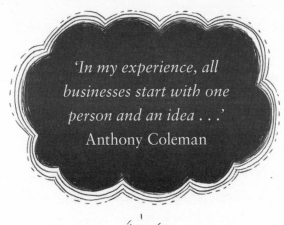

'In my experience, all businesses start with one person and an idea . . .'
Anthony Coleman

CHAPTER ONE

# The Idea

If you ask Felix – and a lot of people do – how it all began, he will probably tell you that it started the day he tried to buy a birthday card for his mother.

He had called in at the shop in the Crescent on his way home from school, but been shocked to find that the cheapest card on the racks was £2.15, and all he had in his pocket was £1.73. How anyone, thought Felix, could charge £2.15 for a bit of stiff paper and an envelope was a mystery, but it was while he was wondering what he should do, that he remembered Mo.

Mo made her own birthday cards. Usually, she drew

them individually, but a few days before she had scanned some of her designs onto the computer, so that she could print one off whenever she needed. If she could print one for him, Felix thought, he would not only have a birthday card for his mother, he would still have his £1.73.

Mo lived in the same road as Felix, three houses further down, so calling at her house was simple enough, but she had been off sick the last two days, and he had to ring the bell several times before she eventually answered the door, dressed in pyjamas, and with a duvet wrapped around her shoulders.

'I know you're not well, and I am *really* sorry to bother you' – Felix held up his hands in an apologetic gesture – 'but is there any way you could print off one of those cards you did? It's for Mum's birthday.'

Mo stared at him through red-rimmed eyes. 'What . . . now?'

'Well . . . fairly soon.' Felix made an apologetic face again. 'She'll be home in about an hour, you see.'

'It's her birthday today?'

'Yes,' said Felix. 'And I know I should have thought of this, like, yesterday or something, but Dad only reminded me this morning, and—'

He stopped, because Mo had turned on her heel and was walking back down the hall and into the living room.

2

Closing the front door behind him, Felix followed her.

The computer was at the far end – this was still a time when most families only had one computer, which everyone shared – and Mo picked up a pile of disks. Shuffling through them, she selected one and passed it to Felix.

'If I give you this, can you print it yourself?'

'No problem. That's great.' Felix took the disk.

'Look . . . is there anything you need? You know . . . anything I can get for you?'

'Short of a magic potion, I'm afraid not.' Mo was already heading back out to the hall. 'But thanks for asking. If you don't mind, I'm going back to bed now. Just print whatever you want.'

His mother liked the card every bit as much as Felix had hoped.

The one he had printed from the five that Mo had given him was a pen-and-ink drawing of a class of school children playing in the woods. They were busily starting fires, falling out of trees and throwing home-made spears at each other, while their teacher, an elderly man in a suit, lay sleeping on the ground. Underneath were the words: *Halfway through a Nature Walk, Mr Wilkins always insisted that 5FW lie down and have a rest . . .*

'I remember Mr Wilkins!' said Felix's mother, chuckling as she studied the card. 'He took you on his Nature Walks every Friday, didn't he?'

Mr Wilkins had been their Year Five teacher at Junior school and had indeed, weather permitting, taken them out into the woods every Friday afternoon. And he had always insisted they take a rest halfway through, though everyone knew that the only person who actually needed it was Mr Wilkins himself. On one famous occasion he had fallen asleep so deeply that he had had to be woken up and told that it was past going-home time.

'He was quite a character, wasn't he?' said Felix's father, when his wife passed him the card. 'Whatever happened to him?'

'Miss Tindall persuaded him to retire,' said William, Felix's older brother. 'He does birdwatching tours with old age pensioners now. He makes them have a rest as well.'

He passed the card to his grandmother, who studied it admiringly.

'It's beautifully drawn, isn't it!' she said, and then peered at the back. 'Where did you get it?'

Felix explained that it had been drawn by a friend, and then printed off on the family's computer.

'Would your friend mind if you printed some for me?'

asked his grandmother. 'Only when I try and buy a card in the shops these days, they're all either too rude or everyone's already seen them.'

Felix remembered that Mo had told him to print whatever he wanted.

'Yes, of course,' he said, and went back to the dining room where he printed off one each of the five designs, folded them, found some envelopes, and brought them back to his grandmother.

She was delighted and, reaching into her purse, took out a five-pound note. Felix assured her it wasn't necessary, but she insisted he take it.

'They'd cost me twice as much in a shop,' she said, 'and they wouldn't be half as good. You take the money.'

So he did.

After the weekend, Felix's grandmother rang to say she had been having tea with two of her friends on Sunday, and had shown them the cards Felix had printed for her.

'They were so impressed,' she said, 'that they'd like some for themselves. Could you do ten each for both of them? And I'll have another five myself if that's all right.'

She called in half an hour later to pick up the cards, and gave Felix twenty-five pounds. Again, he tried to tell her that the money wasn't necessary, but his grandmother pushed the notes into his hands.

'When you get to my age,' she said, 'you're sending out cards all the time. And it's wonderful to have some that you know nobody else has seen. As far as I'm concerned we're getting a bargain.'

So, again, Felix took the money.

Two days after that, as he was leaving school, Felix was stopped outside the main gates by the mother of one of the boys in his class.

'Is it you that's been selling these?' she asked, holding up one of Mo's cards.

Felix had no idea where she had got the card from, or how she knew he was the one who had printed it, but he admitted that, yes, he probably was.

'You do them in packets of ten, don't you?' said the woman, reaching into her purse and taking out a ten-pound note. 'Could I have them tomorrow?'

Felix did not hesitate. 'Sure,' he said. 'No problem.'

And he took the ten pounds.

Which is why, if you ask Felix how the idea of setting up in the card business first came to him, he will tell you the idea never really *came* to him at all. It more sort of jumped up and grabbed him by the throat.

6

After all, when people kept coming up to you and *giving* you money . . .

It was a no-brainer, really.

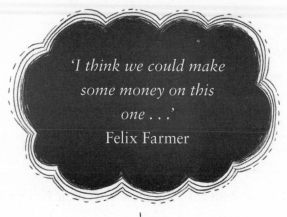

*'I think we could make some money on this one . . .'*

Felix Farmer

CHAPTER TWO

# The Deal

Mo was off school all that week, and it was Saturday before Felix was finally allowed to visit her. He found his friend still in bed, but looking considerably better than the last time he had called.

'I've been trying to see you for days,' he said. 'Your mum wouldn't let me in.'

'I know,' said Mo. 'They thought I might have meningitis.'

'Oh . . .' Felix had no idea what meningitis was, but it sounded serious. 'You haven't, have you?'

'No. Turned out it was just some fluey virus.'

'Ah.' Felix nodded. 'Good.'

Mo smiled. 'So what did you want, Felix? Apart from worrying about how I was.'

'Well . . .' Felix sat himself on the edge of the bed. 'I wanted to tell you about the card you gave me for Mum's birthday.'

'Oh yes? Which one did you use?'

'The one with Mr Wilkins asleep on the Nature Walk.'

'Did she like it?'

'She thought it was great. Everyone did. Gran liked it so much she asked me to do some for her. So I printed off one of each of the cards, and she gave me five pounds.'

Mo looked at him. 'Five pounds?'

'Yes. Then she rang up next day and asked for five more, and she had these friends who wanted some as well, so I did ten each for both of them, and she paid me for those. Then on Wednesday, Dylan's mum stopped me after school and asked if—'

'How much?' interrupted Mo.

'What?'

'How much money have you made?'

'Forty,' said Felix. He reached into his pocket and took out a little fold of banknotes.

'You got forty pounds?' said Mo. 'Selling my cards?'

'Well, it's not *me* that's got it, is it?' said Felix. 'I mean,

9

they're your cards, so obviously the money belongs to you really, but' – he paused – 'I did think, as I was the one that sold them and did the printing and stuff, that maybe we could share the profits. You know. Half and half.'

Mo considered this. 'OK,' she said, eventually. 'Twenty pounds each then, yes?'

'Yes,' said Felix.

Mo waited for him to pass over her share of the money, but he didn't.

'The thing is,' said Felix, 'I was thinking . . . if I could sell forty cards, without even trying, maybe I could sell more. Maybe I could print off, you know, like a couple of hundred, and sell them. But to do that I'd need to buy card and envelopes and printer ink . . . because I've used up most of what we've got at home.'

'And how much would that cost?' asked Mo.

'About forty pounds,' said Felix.

'I thought it might.' Mo looked regretfully at the banknotes Felix was still holding. 'You're sure, are you?'

'About what?'

'About being able to sell more cards.' Mo made a little gesture with her hands. 'I mean, supposing you don't?'

'If I don't,' Felix admitted, 'we'll have lost forty pounds, but I think we could make some money on this one. Really, I do.'

It was not the first time Mo had heard her friend use those words or something similar, but she did not say so. Instead, she simply nodded.

'OK,' she said.

'Great!' Felix stood up, stuffing the banknotes back into his pocket. He headed for the door, but turned before he left. 'I've got a good feeling about this one, Mo,' he said. 'A *really* good feeling!'

Mo watched him go and smiled. The two of them had been friends for as long as she could remember and, when Felix came up with one of his 'ideas', she usually went along with it.

You never knew, one day one of them might actually work.

In the card that Mo had drawn, with Mr Wilkins asleep on the grass, the children were as easily recognizable to anyone from 5FW as their teacher. The boy examining a nest of vipers, for instance, was obviously Barry – who had once brought a pet tarantula into school. The boy shooting himself in the foot with a home-made arrow was the notoriously accident-prone Dylan – who had managed to staple his tongue to the roof of his mouth not once, but twice. And the character down in one corner, who had set up a stall selling cups of soup to his classmates, was obviously Felix. He was to be found in all the cards, and in all of them he was selling something. Because everyone knew that's what Felix did.

Over the years, he had thought up a good many schemes to sell things, and Mo had been at least partly involved in most of them. His first business venture, at the age of six, had been selling bunches of flowers door to door down the street, and she had been responsible for making and carrying the 'bouquets'. In the six years since, Felix had set up more 'businesses' than she could count.

He had sold home-made cakes from a table on the pavement, sold biscuits in the school playground at break, run a second-hand toy exchange from his garage, sold baby mice and rats that he had attempted to breed himself, walked dogs, mowed lawns, and set up a mobile phone renting service for people at school who didn't have one. He had done people's shopping, run competitions and raffles, offered a hair-colouring service, a pet-a-puppy service, a 'homework assistance scheme', and . . .

. . . And sadly, few of these ideas had been what you could call a success. Most had actually lost money rather than made a profit, and two of them had resulted in visits from the police.

Which was why Felix decided, as he walked home

from the shops with a bag containing two hundred and fifty sheets of card, ten packets of envelopes and an alarmingly expensive ink cartridge, that he would only tell his parents about his plan to sell Mo's cards when, or if, the idea succeeded. If it all went nowhere – and he knew perfectly well that it might – he did not want his parents explaining, yet again, how much more sensible it would have been to keep the money in a savings account and not waste it trying to sell things to people who didn't want to buy them.

Luckily, his parents were both busy in the garden when he got home, so neither of them noticed as Felix let himself in the front door, carried the bag upstairs and stowed it carefully in a suitcase under his bed.

He had thought that he might have to wait until Monday before being able to do the printing, but he was lucky about that too. Felix's mother was a veterinary nurse, and was called out after lunch on Sunday to help in an emergency operation on a cat that had been run over by a bicycle. His father, who worked as a supervisor for the Forestry Commission, had already announced that he would be going into the office that afternoon to catch up on some paperwork, and when his brother, William, told him he was going to the cinema, Felix discovered he would have the house to himself all afternoon. Plenty of time in which to print whatever he wanted, undisturbed.

It took a little over an hour to run off forty copies each of the five designs that Mo had given him, then fold them, place them under the flap of an envelope, and sort them into piles of ten. He put each pile in a plastic bag he got from a roll of freezer bags in the kitchen, and carried them upstairs to his bedroom, where he placed them on the floor, sat on the bed, and looked at them.

Two hundred cards, in twenty packets of ten.

All he had to do now, he thought cheerfully, was sell them.

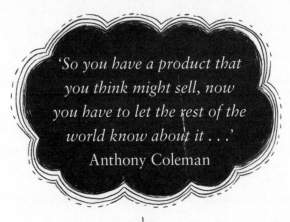

## CHAPTER THREE

# Marketing

There were several methods of selling that Felix was not allowed to use. The police had told him he could not sell things on the street or in any public place without a licence. The school had told him he was not allowed to sell anything to anybody on school premises, and his parents had made him promise not to go up and down the street knocking on people's doors. Apparently some of the neighbours did not like it and had complained.

It didn't leave him many options, Felix thought, but there was one idea he had found in a book that Mo had given him for Christmas. It was called *Everything You*

*Need To Know About Setting Up Your Own Business* by Anthony Coleman. Mo had picked it up from the book stall at the school fete, and Felix had read it twice, from cover to cover.

Chapter Five was entitled *Marketing*, and although a good chunk of it was concerned with the importance of being clean and neatly dressed when you called at a customer's house – something that was not really relevant for Felix – there was a section at the end on advertising, with an idea that he thought might actually work.

'*Another good way to promote your business,*' Anthony Coleman had written, '*is to have a flyer printed outlining your service, and giving a telephone number. The flyer should be bright and cheerful and can be put through the doors of all the houses in your neighbourhood.*'

He had promised his parents not to knock on anyone's door, Felix thought, but posting something through people's letter boxes would not involve any knocking. In school the next morning, during a history lesson, he mapped out a simple design, and in computer science that afternoon managed to put it all together on the screen.

At the top, it said: *Ten Cards for £10!* Underneath, he had scanned-in a picture of one of Mo's cards, and at the bottom he put a couple of sentences explaining that you could buy a selection of brilliant cards like this –

two each of five magnificent designs for a mere £10 – by phoning the number below. Then he gave the number of his mobile.

Felix printed off a hundred copies when he got home and made his first deliveries the next day. He pushed fifty flyers through the letter boxes of two streets of houses on his way to school, and then did the same thing – to fifty different houses in different streets – on the way back.

In the week that followed, however, nobody rang up to order any cards, and when Felix delivered the flyers to another hundred houses a week later, there were no replies from that, either.

It was, he had to admit, disappointing.

Despite this setback, Felix did in fact sell almost all of the two hundred cards he had printed. He sold two more packs of ten to his grandmother, who was still passing them round to her friends, but the others were all sold to people who, like Dylan's mother, stopped him at the school gates and asked for them.

The parents of the children who had been in 5FW at Monmouth Junior liked seeing drawings of teachers they had known, like Mr Wilkins, and they particularly liked recognizing their own children and their children's friends. Felix was stopped so often outside the school gates that he started bringing packs of the cards into school with him, so that he could hand them over on the spot instead of promising to bring some in the next day.

Within the space of a fortnight, he had managed to sell seventeen of the twenty packs he had printed, and made a profit of a hundred and seventy pounds. It was a good result, but Felix was not sure it was worth printing any more. Most of the parents who were going to buy a pack had probably done so by now and the lack of response to any of his flyers was not encouraging.

Then, on Wednesday, a woman called Mrs Melho called him over as he was leaving school and asked if he had 'any of those cards you've been selling'.

Felix said he had, and took a pack out of his bag to show her.

Mrs Melho looked through the cards, and chuckled as she pointed to one of them. 'Ah, there she is, look! There's Samar!'

The picture she was pointing to was one of Felix's favourites. It showed a school playground with a small woman in a black dress in the foreground talking to a man in a suit. Anyone from Monmouth Junior would instantly have recognized the woman as Miss Tindall, the head teacher.

Underneath the picture were the words: *When the*

*Inspector asked how many teachers worked at the school,*
*Miss Tindall said she thought about half . . .*

Behind the head teacher, scattered around the play-ground, were various children from 5FW and one of them was a beautiful girl, with a serene expression, surrounded by a group of boys with their tongues hanging out. The girl was Mrs Melho's daughter, Samar.

'They're such brilliant cards!' Mrs Melho was reaching into her bag for her purse. 'I tried to order some online last night but I couldn't get through.'

'I'm sorry?' said Felix.

The woman pointed to the back of the card where, amongst all the other things Mo had drawn to make the card look like something you might buy in a shop, was printed a bar code and the words *www.thekardmart. co.uk*

'I tried the website several times,' said Mrs Melho, as she handed over a ten-pound note, 'but it didn't seem to work.'

'It's not a real address,' Felix explained. 'Mo just put that on to make it look like it came from a real business.'

But it occurred to him, as he said it, that it might be a good idea if it *was* a real address.

The internet . . . He had a feeling that might be a really good way to sell the cards.

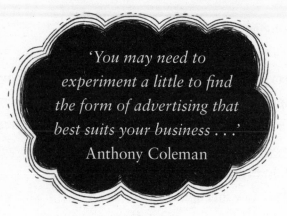

CHAPTER FOUR

# The Website

'One hundred and eighty pounds?' said Mo. 'Seriously?'

'Yes,' said Felix.

The two of them were sitting facing each other on the floor of Mo's bedroom, with Felix holding a clump of banknotes.

'So that's . . . ninety pounds each?'

'Yes.'

'Wow!' Mo grinned. 'That is . . . more than I expected!' She waited for Felix to hand over her share, but he didn't.

'The thing is,' said Felix, 'I think we could make more than that.'

'Oh.' Mo's smile faded. 'Do you?'

Felix told her about Samar's mother and the website address and how it had given him the idea of selling the cards on the internet.

'Are you allowed to?' asked Mo. 'I mean, don't you have to be over twenty-one or something?'

'I don't know,' said Felix.

'And how much will it cost?'

'I don't know that either.'

'And who are you going to get to build the website? Because you don't know anything about computers, do you?'

'No,' said Felix, 'but I thought maybe we could get Ned to do it.'

'Ned Peterson?'

Felix nodded.

Ned Peterson certainly knew about computers. He was the sort of boy, even at Junior school, that teachers turned to when they couldn't work PowerPoint, or their laptops had mysteriously frozen. He was one of those people who only had to sit down and tap at the keyboard for a minute or so and, somehow, everything would start working again. In Mo's drawings, whatever else was happening in the classroom or the playground, or on the Nature Walk, Ned Petersen was to be seen, ignoring everyone else and staring at a computer screen.

'I know he's a friend,' said Mo, 'but he's kind of busy these days, and building a website would mean a lot of work, wouldn't it?'

Felix agreed that it probably would. 'We'd have to pay him something, I expect.' He paused and then added, 'Maybe give him a share of the profits.'

'Ah . . .' Mo leaned back against the side of the bed and looked sadly at the money in Felix's hand. 'I get the feeling I'm not going to get my ninety pounds, am I?'

'Well, you *could* have it now,' Felix assured her. 'I mean, it's your money. But at the moment I don't know how much it'd cost to set up a website, and we're going to have to buy more paper and envelopes and ink and stuff, so . . . it might be best if I hung on to it until we know how much we're going to need. If that's all right?'

Mo sighed.

'I think we could make a lot of money on this one,' said Felix. 'I've got a really good feeling about it.'

'I thought you might,' said Mo, and she looked across at him and smiled. 'OK. Let's go for it!'


Ned was, as Mo had said, busy these days. The three of them had been good friends at Monmouth Junior, but the demands for Ned's computer skills had increased considerably once they moved to secondary school, and

Felix had seen a lot less of him recently. He eventually tracked him down at lunchtime the next day in the lighting control room of the school theatre, during a rehearsal of *Joseph and the Amazing Technicolor Dreamcoat*. The lighting was all controlled by a computer.

'I know you're busy,' said Felix, pulling up a chair to sit beside Ned, 'so just one quick question. How difficult is it to set up a website?'

'What sort of website?' asked Ned, his eyes fixed on the stage visible through the glass in front of him.

'I suppose what I need to know is whether I can set up a website with this address.' Felix held out a piece of paper with *www.thekardmart.co.uk*, written on it, and Ned glanced at it briefly.

'It depends,' he said.

'On what?'

'On whether anyone else has already registered that name. If they have, then you can't. If they haven't, then you can register it yourself.'

'And how much would it cost?' asked Felix. 'To register.'

Ned gave a shrug. 'It varies.'

'Could you find out? Exactly?'

'Probably . . .' Ned glanced across at his friend. 'I'll try and check it out this evening, but at the moment I'm supposed to be—'

'Where are the lights!' shouted Miss Richards from a front seat in the theatre. 'We don't have any lights on Pharaoh! The poor boy can't see a thing!'

'Sorry, Miss Richards!' said Ned, tapping hurriedly at the keyboard.

'That'd be great.' Felix placed the piece of paper carefully on the side of the lighting board. 'You won't forget, will you? Only it's important!'

Ned did not forget, and at lunch break the next day, sitting in the dining hall eating his sandwiches, he told Felix and Mo that the domain name *thekardmart.co.uk* had not yet been registered by anyone else, and that they could set up a site with that address if they wanted.

'It'll cost you thirty pounds,' he said. 'That gives you the rights to the name for two years. Then, if you want it longer than that, you have to pay again.'

Thirty pounds was, if anything, considerably cheaper than Felix had expected. It would mean they could afford to pay to register the name and still buy a fresh supply of stationery and ink.

Which only left two small problems . . .

'Could you do it for us?' asked Felix.

'What?'

'Register the name.'

'I haven't got thirty pounds,' said Ned.

'It's all right,' Mo told him. 'We'll give you the money.'

'You will?'

'Felix has been selling these cards I drew. He's sold a hundred and eighty in the last three weeks. At a pound each.'

'Really?' Ned looked across at Felix, who nodded.

'And I could sell a lot more,' Felix said confidently, 'if we had a website.' He took a set of the cards from his bag and pushed them across the table. 'They are very good!'

Ned studied the card on top of the pile. It was the one of Mr Wilkins, and his attention was drawn to a little figure in the foreground, sitting with his back to a tree, studying a computer screen.

'Is that me?'

'Yes.' Mo nodded. 'You're in most of them.'

'So will you do it?' asked Felix.

'What?'

'Register the name. If we give you the money.'

'Oh.' Ned thought for moment. 'Yes. OK.'

'And the other thing we'll need,' said Felix, 'is some-one to build the website for us.'

'Ah . . .' Ned frowned. 'I'm not sure that—'

'It's all right!' Felix reassured him. 'It won't be any-thing complicated, and we'll tell you what to write. I've worked out what we need to say and Mo's done the design. All you'll have to do is copy it all into, you know, computery language.'

'I am kind of busy at the moment,' said Ned. 'I've got this play and I've got—'

'And in return, you'll get a share of the profits.'

'Any money we make from selling the cards,' said Mo, 'you'll get the same as we do.'

'What if there aren't any profits?'

'Then you don't make anything, and nor do we,' said Felix. 'But if they *did* sell, you could make quite a lot of money.'

'Felix has got a really good feeling about this one,' said Mo.

Ned picked up the cards and riffled through all five. 'They are quite good, aren't they?' he said.

'Those cards,' said Felix, 'are *very* good. I can't guarantee we'll make anything, but I think it's worth a try. And all you have to do is set up the site, then sit back and wait for your share of the money to come in.'

Ned sat in silence for what felt like a long time, before finally looking up at the others.

'All right,' he said with a grin. 'I'm in.'

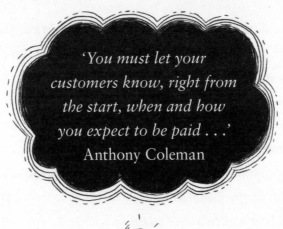

*'You must let your customers know, right from the start, when and how you expect to be paid . . .'*
Anthony Coleman

CHAPTER FIVE

# Going Online

The trickiest part of designing the website, and the problem Felix found hardest to resolve, was working out how people should pay for the cards once they had decided to buy them.

Shopping on the internet, he knew, was mostly done using a credit card, but as Felix did not have a bank account, he would have to ask customers to pay in cash. And his first difficulty was deciding whether he should ask them to pay before he sent them the cards, or after.

Talking about it to Mo, there seemed to be drawbacks to both alternatives. If he asked them to pay in advance, it would inevitably put a lot of people off. Who, after all, would want to send ten pounds to someone they didn't know and who might never reply? On the other hand, if he asked people to pay *after* they had received the cards, how could he be sure they would ever bother to send him the money?

In the end, it was a paragraph in the book Mo had given him for Christmas that helped Felix decide. In *Chapter 8, Finance and Pricing*, Anthony Coleman explained that small traders often had to do the work before they were paid, and that this carried a certain amount of risk.

'*However*,' he wrote, '*this risk is something you have to accept, and is not as high as you might think. Most of your customers will happily pay for the work you have done but, as a rough rule of thumb, about 5% may not. It is important to allow for the fact that about one customer in twenty will, for whatever reason, be reluctant or unable to pay.*'

If it was only one person in twenty that didn't pay, Felix thought, he could probably cope.

After looking at a good many websites online, Felix had made his as simple as possible. There was a 'home' page that said there were cards for sale, a second page that showed what the cards were, and a third where you could fill in your name and address if you wanted to buy some.

Simple as it was, however, the website took most of three weekends and several evenings to build. They did the work at Ned's house, because his computer had the software they needed, and doing it was more fun than any of them had expected. Privately, Ned didn't think the scheme was likely to make any money – Felix's schemes rarely did – but he had never built a website before, found it an interesting challenge, and the end result looked, though he said it himself, quite professional.

For the opening page, Mo had drawn some of the figures from the 5FW classroom to put as a sort of border round the screen. The name of the site – *Kardmart* – ran along the top, looking as if someone had sprayed it there with an aerosol can, and underneath, in a cheery and brightly coloured font, were the words:

*Hi! If you're looking for a greetings card that's a bit different and half the price of cards in the shops, you've come to the right place! Mo Burnley's designs have already won several awards and are hugely popular. Click here and see why!*

Mo was not sure they ought to claim that she had 'won several awards', but Felix pointed out that she had won the school art prize three years running at Monmouth Junior, and she eventually agreed to leave the wording as it was.

When you clicked on *Next*, the screen changed to show all five of Mo's cards and, if you clicked on a particular card, it grew in size so that you could see it in close-up.

Beneath the cards, it said:

*We sell these cards in packs of ten that contain two of each brilliant design. Want to buy a pack for the bargain price of £10? Just click on the button!*

Underneath was a big blue circle with *Buy!* written on it, and when you clicked on the circle, the page changed again.

*Wise choice!* said the writing at the top. *All we need now is your name and address!*

Below it were boxes in which customers could type in their details, and a big yellow button beneath that with *Send!* written on it.

When you clicked on *Send!*, your details would automatically be sent to Felix's email address, which Ned had set up for him on the family computer in the dining room at home. Felix was not sure how exactly this had been done – his parents were still cheerily unaware that he even had an email – but Ned seemed to have fixed it without too much difficulty.

On the final page of the website it said:

*Thank you for your order! As long as the Post Office does its stuff, your cards will be with you in two working days!*

Beside it there were a couple more of Mo's drawings of Monmouth Junior students waving goodbye.

'It looks . . .' said Mo, after they had done a final check that everything worked the way it was supposed to. 'It looks *real*, doesn't it!'

And Felix knew what she meant. The website looked good, but the best thing about it from his point of view was that there was nothing in it to make you think it had been set up by three twelve-year-olds. It looked, as far as he could tell, like any other website selling stuff on the internet, and this was exactly what he had wanted.

One of the difficulties Felix had always faced when trying to sell things in the past was that because, in most people's eyes, he was still a child, they mostly treated him like one. But with the website, nobody ever knew how old he was. The site simply said there were cards for sale, and the age of the person selling them didn't come into it.

'How long before we get it up and running?' he asked.

Ned leaned forward and pressed a couple of keys.

'That's it,' he said. 'It's there.'

For a long moment, nobody spoke.

'So what do we do now?' asked Mo, eventually.

'I think all we do now,' said Felix slowly, 'is wait.'

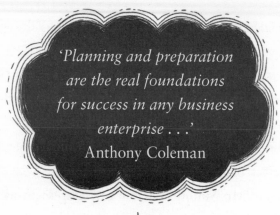

'Planning and preparation
are the real foundations
for success in any business
enterprise . . .'
Anthony Coleman

CHAPTER SIX

# Internet Sales

Every afternoon, the first thing Felix did when he got back
from school was log in to his email account on the computer
in the dining room, and check if there were any orders.

Every afternoon, however, his inbox was empty.

Empty, that is, until the Monday two weeks after the
website was launched, when he came home and found an
order for ten cards from a Mrs Summers in Scarborough.

How Mrs Summers had stumbled across the website,
he never knew, but staring at the screen, Felix felt a small
shiver of excitement. It might only be one order, and Mrs
Summers might turn out to be one of those people who

never actually paid but, deep in his bones, he had the strong conviction that this was an important occasion.

He stood up and headed for the stairs. He'd had several weeks to work out what needed to be done next, and his plans had been carefully laid.

First, he collected a padded envelope from the suitcase under his bed – he had bought a box of twenty – and wrote out Mrs Summers' name and address on the front. Inside it, he placed a pack of Mo's cards, and a slip of paper on which were printed the words:

*We hope you are pleased with your purchase of these cards from Kardmart. If you have any problems, do let us know, but if you are as delighted as we think you'll be, please put a ten-pound note in the envelope provided and pop it in the post. That way we'll be pleased as well!*

Felix had printed out twenty of these slips, ready to use.

The last thing that went in was a brown envelope addressed to Felix himself, with a stamp already attached. In *Everything You Need to Know About Setting Up Your Own Business*, Anthony Coleman had said that if you wanted someone to pay you promptly, it was important to make the process as easy as possible.

Before he put in the envelope, he wrote the number 1, with a circle round it, in pencil in the top left-hand corner. This was so that he would know, when the money was posted back to him, that it had come from Mrs Summers. The envelope he put in with the next order would have a number 2 on it and so on.

After sealing the padded envelope, he took out an exercise book, in which he had already drawn up five columns, and wrote the number '1' in the first column, Mrs Summers' name in the next, the date in the third, and then a tick in the fourth column which meant he had packed up the cards to send to her. The last column would be where he would put another tick when she had sent him the money.

Finally, he put a stamp on the padded envelope, marked it first-class, and there it was, ready for him to put in the post on his way to school the next morning, and all done before his mother got home and found him downstairs, busily doing his homework.

The news that there had been an order was greeted with some excitement by the others the next day. Neither Mo nor Ned had quite believed that anyone would find the website or, even if they did, use it to order any cards. Mrs Summers, however, was not the only one to prove them wrong. There were no emails asking for cards on Tuesday, but there were two more on Wednesday, and one more on Friday.

Felix had a brief moment of worry that maybe no one would pay for the cards he was sending out, but on Thursday, when he got back from school, there was a brown envelope sitting on the doormat with the number 1 written in the top left-hand corner. Inside, there was a ten-pound note and a slip of paper with the words *Such lovely cards. Thank you!* written on it.

He took the money upstairs and put it in an old shoe-box he had been using to keep all the business records. Then he took out the exercise book recording his orders and, with some satisfaction, put a tick under the 'Paid' column next to Order Number 1.

In the week that followed, there were seven more orders for cards and, the week after, another eleven. The week after that, there were thirteen.

Felix reported the news of each sale to the others – it was, understandably, the first thing they wanted to know when he got to school – but it was not until towards the end of the fourth week, by which time the website had received more than thirty orders, that Mo broached the subject of what was obviously the next step.

'So when do we start sharing out the money?' she asked as she and Felix walked home together from school.

'Yes,' said Felix. 'I've been thinking about that.'

'Because you must have got, what . . . about two hundred pounds by now?'

Felix agreed that he had at least that much. 'And we *could* share it out,' he went on, 'except for one problem.'

'Problem?' said Mo. 'You're not going to tell me you want to spend it all on something else, are you?'

'No, it's not that . . .'

'So what sort of problem is it?'

'Well,' said Felix, 'if you've got a moment, I'll show you.'

They had arrived at his front door and, when he pushed it open, he paused to scoop up two brown envelopes that were waiting for him on the mat, before leading Mo upstairs to his bedroom.

In his room, he reached under the bed, pulled out the suitcase, and took out the shoebox he was using to keep the money in and two exercise books.

'In here' – Felix held up one of the exercise books – 'is where I write down all the stuff I've spent money on – stamps, envelopes, paper and so on.' He picked up the second exercise book. 'And this is where I write down all the orders and the money that comes in. What I *ought* to be able to do is add up how much I've spent, how much money has come in, and the difference between those two should be the same as how much money is in there.'

He lifted the lid of the shoebox and gestured to the pile of ten-pound notes, loose change and receipts inside.

'And . . . ?'

'And it never is. Every time I do it, it adds up to something different.'

Felix had in fact done the calculation five times in the last four days, and got a slightly different total each time. Maths had never been his best subject at school, but he found it extremely frustrating that, each time he added up how much he had spent, or how much money was in the box, or how much there *ought* to be in the box, the figures were never quite the same.

'Does it matter?' said Mo. 'I mean, there seems to be plenty of money in the shoebox there. Why don't we just . . . sit down and share it out?'

'I know we could,' said Felix, 'but I really wanted to do it properly this time. The way it's supposed to be done.'

In *Everything You Need to Know About Setting Up Your Own Business*, Anthony Coleman had stated more than once that an important part of running any successful enterprise was keeping an accurate record of exactly how much money came in and went out. Not doing this, he warned, could have serious repercussions further down the line.

Mo briefly considered offering to help count the money

herself but, as her maths scores at school were even worse than Felix's, she quickly dismissed the idea. Then her eye fell on the suitcase, and the packets of cards that Felix kept there, ready to send out. She reached forward, picked up one of the packets and pointed to a figure in the drawing on the front.

'Maybe there's your answer,' she said.

The card was the one of Miss Tindall standing in the playground, and one of the children Mo had drawn was a girl using a piece of chalk on the tarmac to resolve a quadratic equation.

Anyone from Monmouth Junior would have recognized her at once. Ellie-Mae was on several of the cards, and always doing something mathematical. In another of them, Felix remembered, Mo had drawn her using a pen on the classroom wall to calculate the formula for the speed of light.

Ellie-Mae, Felix realized at once, was the perfect answer. She would have no problem sorting out the numbers in the exercise books and how much money was in the box.

When Ellie-Mae added things up, they stayed added, the way they were supposed to.

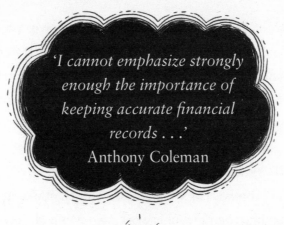

*'I cannot emphasize strongly enough the importance of keeping accurate financial records . . .'*
Anthony Coleman

CHAPTER SEVEN

# Keeping Account

The next day, at lunchtime, Felix found Ellie-Mae in one of the practice rooms in the music centre, playing her cello.

'Hi,' he said, pulling up a chair. 'Sorry to interrupt, but . . . I need your help.'

'We are practising, Felix.' Ellie-Mae gestured with her bow to the three other students in the room. Two of them had violins and one had a flute. 'For the concert.'

'Yes, right, and I'll be as quick as I can . . .' Felix sat himself down beside her. 'You see, there's this business I've started . . .'

'Ah . . .' Ellie-Mae looked at him over the top of her glasses.

She had some experience of Felix's business ventures. He had once persuaded her to play her cello in the high street on a Saturday morning, while he passed round a hat and collected the money. In the half hour before the police arrived, it had been remarkably successful.

'It's all right,' said Felix. 'You won't get arrested this time, I promise. I'm selling these cards that Mo drew, but I'm having a bit of trouble working out exactly how much profit there is. I need to know, so I can share the money with Mo and Ned. Ned built the website, you see.' He paused. 'Could you help?'

'You want me to do your accounts?'

'Yes,' said Felix. 'That's it, exactly. I need you to do the accounts.'

Ellie-Mae nodded. 'OK.'

'Brilliant!' said Felix. 'Is there any chance you could come home with me today after school?'

Mo considered this. 'You are quite sure I will not be arrested?'

'Absolutely positive,' Felix assured her.

'Then I shall see you after school,' said Ellie-Mae.


Ellie-Mae met Felix at the school gates at three thirty. She would probably have been there even if he had told

40

her that there *was* a chance of being arrested again, because . . . well . . . he was Felix.

Ellie-Mae could still remember her first day at Monmouth Junior. She had been eight years old and, until a week before had lived all her life in Hong Kong. Then she had been sent to live with her grandmother in England and, standing in the playground at break time, surrounded by shouting and noise, she had never felt more lonely and frightened in her life.

Until Felix had bustled over and, before she knew it, swept her up into a game of statues that he was organizing. In a way, he had been sweeping her up into things ever since. They were not always the sort of things her grandmother would have approved of, if she had known about them, but they had meant she was hardly ever frightened and never lonely.

They had, from that first day, been firm friends, and although they saw rather less of each other these days because they were mostly in different classes, when Felix asked for her help, Ellie-Mae did not hesitate.

Walking home, he explained to her about the card business and how it had, to his surprise, been more successful than most of his other ventures. When, up in his room, he showed her the contents of the shoebox, Ellie-Mae was surprised as well.

'You have made all this money,' she said, staring at the ten-pound notes mixed in with the receipts, 'from selling cards?'

'That's right.' Felix pulled out the two exercise books and passed them across. 'This one is the list of all the people that bought them – the tick there means they've paid – and this other book's got a list of all the stuff I've had to buy. It's a bit untidy, but I think everything's there. All I need is for someone to make the numbers add up right.'

Ellie-Mae nodded. Her fingers were already reaching into the box, taking things out and putting them in separate piles – shop receipts in one, banknotes in another, coins in a third.

'Do you mind if I leave you to it?' said Felix, after watching her for a moment. 'Only there's stuff I need to do on the computer before my parents get home.' He gathered up some envelopes and packets of cards, and stood up. 'Give a shout if you need anything.'

Downstairs, checking his emails, Felix found he had two more orders, one from North London and the other from Stafford. He set about writing the addresses on a couple of padded envelopes, and putting a packet of cards and a reply envelope in each.

Ten minutes later, with both envelopes stamped, sealed

and ready for the post the next day, he went back upstairs to write the orders in the exercise book he had left with Ellie-Mae, and found she had made excellent progress.

The receipts were all in a pile on the carpet in front of her, held together with paper clips. The banknotes were neatly bundled into rolls tied up with rubber bands, the spare coins – the change from Felix's various shopping trips – were in a plastic bag, and Ellie-Mae was carefully writing something in a little notebook.

'I will need,' she said, pointing to the exercise books and the receipts, 'to take these home with me.'

'OK,' said Felix. 'I'll just fill in today's stuff before you go, shall I?'

He began writing up the new orders, while Ellie-Mae carefully replaced the money in the shoebox.

'Any idea how long it'll take?' he asked. 'I mean, could you have it done by Monday?'

'Monday . . .' Ellie-Mae was carefully packing everything into her school bag. 'Yes. That will be all right.'

'Fantastic,' said Felix. 'Couldn't be better.'

Ellie-Mae was as good as her word. In the library at break on Monday she showed Felix an accounts book – where she had got it from he did not know – with all the details of his card business neatly copied out on the first few pages. The expenses were on the left-hand pages, income on the right, and she explained they would be using separate pages for each month. The receipts were all carefully stored in envelopes, with dates and totals written on the front, and she told Felix he should put these back in the shoebox. She had also written, on a separate piece of paper, what she called a 'running total' of all the income and expenditure so far and exactly how much profit had been made. It came to £324.78.

'That is perfect,' Felix told her, beaming happily. 'I'll show it to Mo and Ned at lunchtime. I think they're going to like it.' He smiled again as he looked at the total. 'I think they're going to like it a *lot*!'

Ned and Mo did indeed like it.

'Three hundred and twenty-four pounds?' said Ned. 'Are you sure?'

'Ellie-Mae did the adding up,' said Felix, 'so, yes, I'm quite sure. But we can't share out all of it yet. I need to keep some of it so I can buy more envelopes and stamps and stuff.'

In his book, Anthony Coleman had stressed the importance of always keeping enough ready cash to cope with emergencies.

'So how much are we going to share?' asked Mo.

'I thought we could give ourselves fifty each to start with,' said Felix. 'That should leave plenty in reserve. Is that OK with you both?'

'It's OK with me,' said Ned. 'When?'

'If you come home after school, we could share it out then,' said Felix. 'And there's one other thing. I think we should give Ellie-Mae a share as well. We're going to need her to keep doing the accounts.'

'How big a share?' asked Ned.

It was a question to which Felix had already given some thought. He knew it would be quite easy to argue that Ellie-Mae's share should be smaller than the others, on the grounds that she had, so far at least, done less work, but he had quickly realized that would not be as simple as it might sound. If you started sharing out the money on the basis of who had done the most work, you could wind up with all sorts of arguments before you found something everyone agreed was fair. In the end, he had decided that the best way of avoiding such disagreements was simply to give everyone the same.

'I think we should give her the same as we're getting,' he said. 'Equal shares keeps it simple.'

'Equal shares is OK with me,' said Mo.

'Me too,' said Ned, still studying the total. 'There seems to be enough to go round.'

'Good,' said Felix. 'That's settled then.'

It was not a decision that he ever regretted.

As he later said, without Ellie-Mae, they would never have survived what happened next.

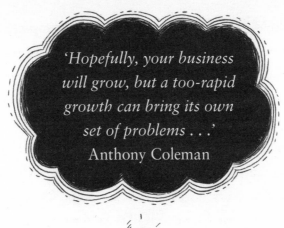

'Hopefully, your business will grow, but a too-rapid growth can bring its own set of problems . . .'
Anthony Coleman

CHAPTER EIGHT

# Increased Sales

For several months, things ran like a dream.

Felix would get home from school, check his email to see if there were any orders and, if there were, pack and address the padded envelopes as required. The next morning he would post them on his way to school, while at weekends he would stock up with stationery. He printed more cards, as they were needed, whenever he had the house to himself.

And the money kept rolling in. Almost every day there would be another brown envelope – or two, or three – lying on the mat when Felix got home from school, and he would take them upstairs and put the ten-pound notes they contained in the shoebox in the suitcase under his bed. Through March they were averaging sales of about a dozen sets of cards a week, and by May it was nearer twenty.

Once a week, Ellie-Mae came home with him after school, gathered up all the receipts, counted the money, and wrote everything down in her accounts book. Every two or three weeks, all four of them would meet at Felix's house and sit in a circle on the floor of his bedroom. Ellie-Mae would read out how much profit they had made, and then solemnly hand out a roll of banknotes – usually something between fifty or a hundred pounds – to each of them.

Ned said it was as if Felix had invented a magic machine that just printed the money. They didn't seem to have to *do* anything to earn it. They didn't advertise the business. They didn't spend any time trying to persuade people to buy the cards, and yet . . . the orders kept coming in. The brown envelopes kept landing on the mat by the front door, and the money kept accumulating in the shoebox until it was time for another share out. It was indeed . . . magical.

Privately, Felix wondered how long it could last. Each day, when he got home, he half expected to find there were no more orders on the computer and no more brown envelopes on the mat. Each day, he knew, the whole thing might end as suddenly and as mysteriously as it had started.

But that wasn't what happened.


Almost as soon as the website had been launched, back in February, Felix had been urging Mo to produce another set of cards. In an ideal world, he thought Kardmart should be producing a new set of cards each month, but it was not until the end of May that Mo finally produced a second set of drawings of 5FW at Monmouth Junior.

They were worth the wait though. They were based this time on school visits – to the zoo, to the museum, to a castle, to the science park and so on – and all the same characters were in them. There was Dylan, managing to electrocute himself on a display of the history of the light bulb, the beautiful Samar was still trailed by a group of admiring boys, and Barry could be seen gazing longingly into a pit of venomous snakes while playing with his pet scorpion.

'Better than ever, Mo,' Felix murmured as he studied them. 'Better than ever!'

Ned put the new cards on the website over the weekend, and Felix sent an email to everyone who had bought the first lot of cards, telling them that new ones were now available – and the result was highly gratifying.

Previously, the highest number of orders Felix had received in one day was six, but the Monday after the new cards went on sale, he came home from school and opened his email to find forty-seven orders waiting for him.

Addressing and sending out forty-seven sets of cards instead of the usual two or three was not easy, but Felix managed it. Luckily, he had printed a particularly large quantity at the weekend – mostly of the new cards – and had built up a healthy stockpile of envelopes and stamps. Even so, packing and addressing that many padded envelopes was a lot to get done, and he only managed it by doing half of them, with Mo's help, in his free time at school the next day.

Then, when he got home on Tuesday, he found a further sixty-three orders waiting for him.

Felix knew there was no way he could fill them – there were only three packs of cards left in the suitcase upstairs – and so he did not try. Instead, he went straight back into town and bought as much card and envelopes as he could carry. That evening, he ate very little supper and went to bed early, muttering that he felt 'a bit off'. The next morning, he announced that he was not feeling well.

'I thought last night you might be going down with something,' said his mother. 'Perhaps you shouldn't go into school today.'

Felix agreed that might be best.

'I'll ring work,' said his mother. 'Tell them I've got to stay home and look after you.'

'I don't think it's that bad,' Felix told her bravely. 'I just feel a bit off. I'm sure I'll be fine with Mrs Button.'

Mrs Button was the old lady who lived next door and was always happy to be on hand if either Mo or Felix were ill. She would pop round during the day to check all was well, and had all the emergency numbers to call if it wasn't.

So his mother went off to work, and Felix spent all of Wednesday printing cards, packing them up and addressing the envelopes to the people who had emailed him the day before, and the thirty-nine *more* people who had placed orders that day. It meant that, by teatime, he had printed and packed up over a thousand cards and it was perhaps not surprising that, when his mother got home, she found him tucked up in bed and fast asleep.

'I don't know what he's got, but the poor boy looks completely worn out,' Mrs Farmer told her husband when he got in from work. 'I think I'll keep him home tomorrow as well. Let him catch up on his rest.'

On Thursday, when Mo called in after school with a further supply of card and envelopes that Felix had requested, he gave her, as he had the day before, two large carrier bags full of padded envelopes to take to the post. There had been another fifty-three orders that day.

'What are you going to do if it carries on like this?' she asked.

'I don't know,' said Felix.

'I mean, you can't keep taking days off school, can you?'

'No.'

Mo watched as Felix fed another stack of card into the printer before setting it going.

'You don't think maybe it's time to tell your parents what's going on?' she said. 'I mean, they're not going to be angry or anything, are they? Because you're making money. A lot of money.'

'I know,' Felix agreed. 'But I still don't want to tell them.'

He was perfectly aware that Mo was right, and that everything would be a lot easier if his parents knew what was going on, but Felix still wanted to avoid telling them about Kardmart if he could. It was *his* business, and he did not want his parents, or anyone else for that matter, giving him advice, or telling him it was taking up too much of his time, or . . . or telling him anything really. Keeping the business a secret was, for Felix, an important part of the magic.

'It's half term next week,' he said. 'I'll be all right then.'

At half term, while the rest of his family were still going out to work each day, Felix would have the house to himself. His parents had a long-standing arrangement with Mo's mother, a school librarian, that in any school holidays she would look after Felix. In the past, that usually meant he would spend the days at Mo's house, but now they were older, Mo's mother did not mind too much which house they spent their time in. The two of them were usually together, but they might be in either house, depending on what they were doing.

'And I doubt it'll go on like this for much longer,' said Felix, pointing to the pile of padded envelopes he had given Mo to post. 'Things'll probably get back to normal soon.'

He was wrong.

On Friday, there were sixty-two orders, which meant that the total for the last five days was two hundred and sixty-four. In the week that followed, there were never less than fifty orders when Felix did his daily check of the computer, and on the Monday – often the busiest day of the week for some reason – there were a hundred and three.

While half term should have made it comparatively easy to fill even this many orders, there was one complication that threatened to upset Felix's plans. He would not, he discovered, have the house entirely to himself after all, because his brother was going to be home all day as well.

William was six years older than Felix, and had suddenly and unexpectedly lost his job – packing tea into boxes – because the factory where he worked was closing down. It was not a job he had enjoyed particularly, but William had not found it easy to get any job after leaving school. In fact, he had been unemployed for several months before finding work packing tea – and the news that he had to begin the process of job-hunting all over again had left him understandably gloomy.

In the event, having his brother at home was less of an inconvenience than Felix might have expected. Wrapped in his own concerns, William was not inclined to show much interest in what his little brother might be doing. He spent most of his time at home either up in his bedroom, or in the kitchen, cooking.

Even so, Felix did not find it easy. The number of orders meant a great deal of work. There was the strain of trying to hide several thousand cards, along with boxes of envelopes and jiffy bags, in his bedroom, and perhaps trickiest of all was the difficulty of making sure no one else noticed the regular arrival of several dozen brown envelopes each day.

It was all getting increasingly complicated, and Felix was beginning to think that Mo was right, and that his parents would have to be told when, on the Friday of half term, two things happened that gave him no choice.

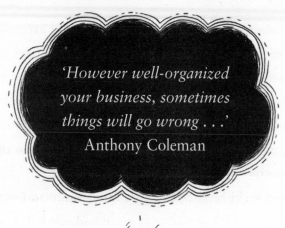

*'However well-organized your business, sometimes things will go wrong . . .'*
Anthony Coleman

CHAPTER NINE

# Crisis

The first thing that happened that Friday was that when Felix walked into town with Mo to buy some more padded envelopes, he found the shop didn't have any.

'We've had a bit of a run on ones that size recently,' said the man behind the counter, when Felix asked why there were none on display. 'They've been very popular, and we've sold out.'

'Are you getting more in?' asked Felix.

'Oh, yes!' said the man. 'Should have them by the middle of next week.'

The middle of next week was too late, Felix thought.

His website promised that his cards would arrive within two working days, and for that to happen he needed the envelopes today or tomorrow at the latest. Anthony Coleman in his book had emphasized more than once that, if you promised to do something in a certain time, the good businessman always carried through on his word.

They tried both of the only other shops in town that sold stationery, but neither of them had padded envelopes of the right size. Walking home, Felix considered his next move. He could, he thought, use an ordinary envelope instead of a padded one, and hope that the cards did not get damaged in the post, but a better option might be to go shopping in Southampton. There were plenty of places there that could provide the envelopes he needed.

'Maybe,' he suggested to Mo, 'you could get your mum to take us.'

'To Southampton?' said Mo. 'I could ask. But she'll want to know why we're going.'

'Couldn't you tell her you wanted to buy clothes or something?'

'I could,' Mo agreed, 'but then when you went off and bought a box of a thousand padded envelopes, she'd probably ask what they were for, wouldn't she? And what would you say?'

When Felix got home, he was still trying to think of an answer to that. Standing by the printer – he thought he might at least print off some more cards while he was working out what to do – he was wondering if it might be possible to hire a taxi, when . . .

'It's not working.'

Felix turned round to find his brother, William, standing in the doorway.

'What?'

'The printer,' said William. 'It's broken. I tried to print off a job application earlier, but when I turned it on, nothing happened.'

Felix tried turning the printer on and off, but his brother was right. No light came on. There was no sound of humming machinery. Nothing. He looked down to see if it was plugged in.

'I checked that,' said his brother. 'I checked everything. It's broken.' He held out a thick wodge of brown envelopes. 'The postman's been. You got forty-seven letters. What's all that about then?'

'Oh . . . nothing.' Felix took the envelopes and headed for the stairs. 'It's a project I'm doing for school.'

Upstairs in his room, he sat on the floor and stared at the wall opposite. If he had no printer, that was it really. He could afford to buy a new one easily enough, but a new printer was not the sort of thing you could bring into the house and hope no one noticed. A new printer would lead to questions like how he could afford to buy it, and what he wanted it for . . .

It was a shame, but there was no way out.

His parents would have to be told.

He waited until they got home, a little after five, and explained that he had something important to tell them.

'Do we have time for a bath first?' asked his father. 'Only I've been winching out tree roots all day, and your mother's been operating on a Labrador with heart trouble.'

'It's all right,' said Felix. 'This won't take long.'

He led the way through to the kitchen, where he had already placed the shoebox from under his bed in the middle of the table. He sat down, and waited for his parents to do the same.

'The thing is,' he said, 'back in January—'

'I knew it!' His mother pointed a finger accusingly at Felix. 'You've started another business, haven't you!'

'Yes,' Felix admitted. 'Back in January—'

'All right!' His father raised his hands in a gesture of defeat. 'What have you done this time?'

'Well,' said Felix, 'back in January—'

'Just don't tell us you owe lots of money to people!' His mother interrupted again. 'I couldn't cope with that. Not at the moment.'

'I don't owe money to anybody!' said Felix. 'I've been making a profit.'

'A profit?' His father looked at him doubtfully. 'Really?'

'Really,' said Felix.

He lifted the lid of the shoebox, took out Ellie-Mae's account book, and pushed it across the table towards his parents.

'You can see for yourself.' He flipped open the book. 'It's all in here. But the problem is, although I've got all these orders, I can't send anyone the cards they want, because the shop's run out of the envelopes I need. And today I found the printer's broken, so . . .'

He stopped, because neither of his parents were listening. Nor were they looking at the accounts book. Instead, they were both staring, open-mouthed, at the shoebox, which was filled to overflowing with ten-pound notes.

'Where did all this money come from?' asked his father.

'I'm trying to tell you,' said Felix. 'It's from the business I set up. We sell these cards and—'

'How much have you *got* in here?' His mother had taken a handful of banknotes and lifted them up . . . to find more banknotes underneath, some of them in the neat hundred-pound rolls that Ellie-Mae had left from her last visit.

'I'm not sure,' said Felix, wondering if he would ever get his parents to concentrate on what he was saying. 'I think it's a bit over four thousand pounds, but what I need is for—'

'*Four thousand pounds?*' His father stared at him. 'You're saying you've made . . . *four thousand pounds?*'

'Well,' said Felix, 'if you look at the account book you'll see it's a bit more than that. But we've been sharing some of it out each month, so . . .'

He stopped again, because they still weren't listening. His father had picked up one of the ten-pound notes and was examining it as if he weren't quite sure it was real.

His mother recovered first. 'And when, exactly, were you planning to tell us about all this?' she demanded.

'Well, I wasn't,' said Felix. 'But I don't have any choice now. You see, I need some help.'

The meal that evening was a little late.

First of all Felix had to tell his parents the whole story. How it had all started with Mo letting him print off the birthday card for his mother, how he had got the idea of selling them, the deal he had made with Mo, getting Ned to do the website – they all went into the dining room at that point to look at it on the computer – and then how Ellie-Mae had been brought in to organize the accounts.

Once his parents were convinced that Felix hadn't actually done anything illegal, or stolen the money from somewhere, they began to relax and even to look quite cheerful, though still clearly astonished. They sat at the kitchen table, poring over the figures in Ellie-Mae's accounts book, shaking their heads in disbelief.

'Do you realize,' said his mother, as she ran her fingers down the columns, 'that you made more money last week than I get in a month?'

'It's not all profit,' said Felix. 'I have to buy stamps and envelopes and stuff. And I share it with the others, remember.'

'In fact your business seems to be making more than your father and I put together.' Mrs Farmer was still not really listening. She smiled at her husband. 'Maybe we should retire and let him look after us.'

It was good that his mother was smiling, Felix thought, but what he really needed was some practical help in getting hold of some padded envelopes and a new printer.

'The thing is,' he said, 'I got all these orders for cards today, but I can't do anything about them unless someone takes me to Southampton tomorrow. So I can get envelopes the right size, and a new printer.'

'Well, we can take you shopping easily enough. No problem there . . .' His father paused for a moment, his forehead furrowed in thought. 'But that might not be the only help you need.'

'Yes, it is,' said Felix. 'Once we've done the shopping, I can get on with sending out the cards.'

'Maybe . . .' His father still had that thoughtful look. 'But I'm not sure it's quite that simple. You see, this isn't just a matter of you earning a bit of extra pocket money.' He reached forward to pick up a clump of the banknotes from the box. 'What you've got here is . . . is a *business*. And there are things you have to do when you set up a business. People you have to tell.'

'Are there? What people?'

'That's the point. I don't know. Because I'm not a businessman. I think you need to talk to someone who is, and get some proper advice.'

'I don't know any businessmen,' said Felix.

'No,' said his father. 'But I do.'

'Goodness!' Felix's mother was staring at him. 'I've just realized what you mean. Do you really think he'd . . .'

'I think it's worth a try.' Felix's father put the banknotes he was holding carefully back in the box. 'Definitely. Worth a try.'

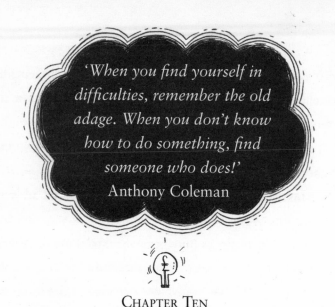

'When you find yourself in difficulties, remember the old adage. When you don't know how to do something, find someone who does!'

Anthony Coleman

CHAPTER TEN

# The Business Consultant

Felix knew that he had an uncle Rufus – there was a photo on the mantelpiece in the front room of Felix's father and his brother, taken when they were both young men – but he had never met him. He had always presumed this was because his uncle lived too far away to visit, and it was a shock to discover that, far from living on the other side of the world, his uncle lived in a village just eight miles away.

'Rufus was a lot like you when he was younger,' his father told Felix as they drove out there the following morning. 'Always coming up with schemes for making money. Ideas for some business or other. When he left school at fifteen, he bought a sponge and a couple of buckets and went round cleaning people's wheelie bins. We all thought he was mad, until we found out how much he was making. Then he got someone else to do the cleaning while he set up a shop that sold T-shirts. After that it was video rentals, then he moved into property . . . I've lost track of what he does now. He's had so many businesses over the years.'

Whatever business his uncle was into these days, Felix thought, it must be doing all right. Rufus Farmer lived in the biggest house Felix had ever seen. They drove up to it through a pair of electric gates, went down a drive lined with trees, and came to a stop in front of a sprawling building set in a couple of acres of lawn that sloped down to a lake.

Pulling up by the steps that led to the front door, Felix's father made no move to get out. Instead, while Felix stared out at the building, he said, 'If your uncle asks why you wanted to see him, there's no need to mention it was me who suggested it.'

'No?'

'No. Just say you were . . . hoping to ask his advice. About whether there's anything you should be doing. That sort of thing.'

'OK,' said Felix.

The front door opened, and Uncle Rufus appeared. He looked like a slightly rounder version of Felix's father, with glasses and less hair, but was still recognizably the same figure as the one in the photo on the mantelpiece at home. He waited by the door without speaking, while Felix and his father got out of the car.

'This is very good of you, Rufus,' said Felix's father. 'I appreciate it.'

Uncle Rufus did not answer, but simply looked at Felix.

There was one of those slightly awkward silences, and Felix realized he had expected his father to walk over and give his brother a hug or shake hands or something . . . but he did neither of those things.

'When shall I come and pick him up?' he asked.

Uncle Rufus glanced at his watch 'Give us an hour. We should be done by then.' He looked at Felix. 'Did you bring the cards?'

Felix had been told that his uncle had asked to see some of the cards he was selling, and the accounts book, so he had brought them both.

'OK.' Uncle Rufus turned towards the house, gesturing for Felix to follow. 'Let's go.'

While his father got back in the car, Felix followed his uncle inside. He led the way across an entrance hall which had two large sofas in front of an enormous fire-place, through a sitting room the size of a tennis court, then through a dining room with chairs round the table for twenty-four people. He walked briskly down a hallway, and finally emerged into a kitchen slightly larger than all the rooms in Felix's house put together.

In the kitchen, a woman with short blonde hair and an even shorter skirt was loading a dishwasher. She gave Felix a nod and a smile, but Uncle Rufus ignored her as he walked straight through and out onto a terrace, where he sat down in one of several large wicker chairs set out round a table and motioned Felix to sit opposite.

Still without speaking, he opened the packet of cards Felix had brought and studied them carefully. Then he opened the accounts book and went through it, his eyes darting up and down the numbers on each page. Finally, he leaned back in his chair, looked across at Felix and, for the first time, there was a faint smile on his lips.

'Impressive,' he said. 'So how did you do it?'

For the second time in two days, Felix found himself telling the story of how he had set up the business selling Mo's cards. His uncle listened intently, only occasionally interrupting with a brief question, while Felix told him about people asking him for cards at the school gates, about persuading Ned to set up a website, about getting

Ellie-Mae to do the accounts, and finally about the sudden explosion of orders that had started two weeks before.

'You know what I really like about all this?' Uncle Rufus had picked up one of the cards again and was staring at it. 'It's the way your business advertises itself. You don't have to tell anyone about your cards, do you? Because your customers do it for you. Every time they buy one and send it out, they're spreading the word. Your business goes all over the country without you lifting a finger!'

Felix had never thought about it quite like this, but it helped explain, he realized, why the orders came in from so many different places.

'And I like the way you brought in the others to help you as well. One of the first rules of business, that. When you don't know how to do something, find someone who does.' Uncle Felix paused and looked across at Felix. 'And you really set all this up on your own? Your parents didn't know about any of it?'

'Not till yesterday,' said Felix. 'And I wouldn't have told them then, but with no envelopes and the printer breaking down I didn't have much choice.'

The smile on his uncle's face broadened. 'I like it!' he said, and then gestured to the accounts book. 'But you seem to be doing all right. What do you want from me?'

'Well,' said Felix. 'Dad says you know everything about setting up a business, and you'd be the one who knew if there's anything I should be doing, or if there's people I should tell, or if I'm making any mistakes.' He paused. 'So I think what I'd like, is just that. To ask if there was anything you thought I should be doing.'

Uncle Rufus considered this for several seconds before answering. 'Two things,' he said. 'Two things you need to be doing – apart from getting a new printer and the envelopes, which I'm sure you can sort out yourself.'

He leaned forward in his chair.

'One, you need to work out a new system for printing the cards and sending them out. It's obviously too much work for you to do on your own, so you'll need to find someone who can help. Whoever you choose, make sure it's someone you can trust, and then keep an eye on them.

'And the second thing,' his uncle continued, 'though I would argue that it's probably the thing you need to do first – is sorting out exactly what sort of a business you have.'

Felix frowned. 'How do you mean?'

'Who owns Kardmart?' said Uncle Rufus. 'At the moment.'

'Well . . .' Felix was about to say that the business belonged to him – it had, after all, been his idea and he had always been the one in charge – but even before he spoke, he realized this wasn't strictly true. Mo had designed the cards, Ned had done the website, Ellie-Mae did the accounts, and they all shared in the profits.

'I suppose we sort of share it,' he said. 'The four of us.'

'So it's a partnership.' His uncle nodded. 'OK. But what sort of partnership? Does one of you have a bigger share than the others?'

'Not really,' said Felix. He explained about sharing out the profits every few weeks. 'I did think about Ellie-Mae not getting as much as the rest of us,' he added, 'but then I realized that would be . . . complicated. We'd have to work out who had done how much work and how much it was worth, and . . . I thought that would just lead to a lot of arguing. And I didn't want to argue. Not with my friends.'

'I can understand that,' said his uncle. 'But it doesn't sound very fair to me. I mean, you're the one who set it all up. It was your idea, and you're the one doing most of the work – and yet you only get the same share as everyone else? Is that fair?'

'Maybe not,' said Felix, 'but I don't see how I can change it now. Like I said, they're my friends.'

'In my experience,' said Uncle Rufus, 'things not being fair can be one of the quickest ways to lose friends.' He gave a little shrug. 'But it's your business and your decision. What you *do* need to do, though, is get it all down on paper. You need to call a meeting of your friends – and they'll need a parent or guardian or whatever to come along as well – and you need to get everyone to agree exactly who owns the business. If you want it to be a partnership of equal shares, that's fine, but you need to get everyone's agreement, and you need to do it soon.'

'If I called a meeting,' said Felix, 'I'm not sure I'd know what to say.'

'It's not really that difficult.' Uncle Rufus smiled at him. 'But if you thought it would help, I'd be happy to come along and chair the meeting for you.'

'You would?' Felix looked up gratefully.

'I don't do that sort of thing for free, of course,' said his uncle. 'I charge a fee.'

'Oh . . . How much?'

'One per cent,' said Uncle Rufus firmly. 'I'd want one per cent of any profits' – he pointed a finger at Felix – 'that you earn.' He paused. '*Your* profits, not the overall profits from the business. But that fee would also entitle you to use me as a consultant. Any time you wanted my advice, you could call me up and ask for it.' He held out a hand. 'Is it a deal?'

Felix did not hesitate. He had a rough idea of what one per cent of his profits would be and had a feeling that, even if it had been twenty times as much, he would still be getting a bargain. He took his uncle's hand and shook it.

'It's a deal,' he said. 'And thank you.'

Shortly after that, the blonde woman in the kitchen – whose name was Ludmila, and who turned out to be Rufus's girlfriend – brought out a large cake, a mug of tea for Uncle Rufus, and a glass of fizzy orange for Felix. As they ate and drank, Uncle Rufus suggested that Felix organize the meeting for early that afternoon.

'No point hanging around,' he said. 'And it's probably easiest if everyone meets at your house. So you need to phone round when you get home, tell your friends what's happened, and say you need them there at, say, two o'clock?'

'What do I do,' asked Felix, 'if one of them says they're busy and can't come?'

'Tell them there's a lot of money to share out,' said Uncle Rufus. 'That usually makes people turn up.' He pulled out a notebook. 'Now, if I'm going to be in charge, I'd better know a bit more about who these people are.'

For the next fifteen minutes, he questioned Felix closely about Mo, Ned and Ellie-Mae, what they had done, what sort of people they were and, in rather more detail, what exactly they had contributed to the partnership.

They were still talking when Ludmila came out with the news that Felix's father had returned.

Felix followed his uncle back through the house to the front door, where he was slightly surprised to find his mother, as well as his father, standing by the car in the drive.

'We've decided there needs to be a meeting,' Uncle Rufus told them briskly. 'The other three partners, and a parent for each of them if possible. Felix is going to invite them round to your house this afternoon.'

'Right . . .' said Felix's father. 'He knows what to do, does he?'

'He's asked me to chair the meeting,' said Uncle Rufus. 'If that's all right with you?'

'Yes, of course,' said Felix's father.

'I'll see you at two o'clock then.'

Uncle Rufus was about to turn and go back into the house when Felix's mother stepped forward and, without a word, put her arms round him and hugged him.

Felix could see the look of surprise on his uncle's face. For a moment, he did not respond, but then he slowly lifted an arm and patted her, a little awkwardly, on the back.

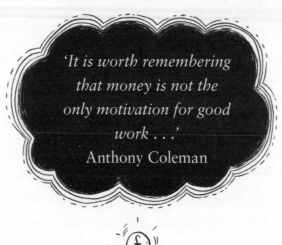

## CHAPTER ELEVEN

# The Board Meeting

'My name,' said Uncle Rufus, looking round at everyone in the room, 'is Rufus Farmer. In case you don't know, I am Felix's uncle. I have a certain amount of business experience, and that is why Felix and his parents have invited me to chair this meeting.'

It was two o'clock that same Saturday, and Uncle Rufus was sitting at the head of the dining-room table in Felix's house. Felix, Mo, Ned and Ellie-Mae were sitting on the other chairs at the table, and behind them, on more chairs spread out along the walls, were all the adults – Felix's mother and father, Mo's mother, Ned's father and

Ellie-Mae's grandmother. Uncle Rufus had been right about one thing, Felix thought. The mention of money had meant that, even with only a few hours' notice, everyone had turned up.

There was an odd atmosphere in the room. Most of the adults had only discovered that day what their children had been up to, and were not quite sure if they should be angry at not being told about it earlier, or pleased at the news of their success. They had all known Felix for a good many years and were, perhaps understandably, a little suspicious of anything he might have got their children involved in.

'You will have heard,' Uncle Rufus continued, 'that earlier this year, your children set up a business, which has turned out to be rather more successful than any of them expected.'

'It's true then, is it?' asked Mo's mother. 'This isn't just one of Felix's . . . ideas?'

'I understand it *was* Felix's idea originally,' said Uncle Rufus, 'but the success is real enough.' He gestured to the shoebox sitting in the middle of the table. 'There is something over four thousand pounds in that box, and one of the things we're here to decide is what to do with it.'

There was a brief silence.

'*How* much?' said Ned's father.

'Something over four thousand pounds,' repeated Uncle Rufus. He looked round at the parents. 'And if you're surprised, you should be. It is a remarkable achievement.'

He gestured to the accounts book on the table. 'I'd like to start off, if I may, by congratulating Ellie-Mae on these accounts here. They are the reason I am able to say so confidently that the money has been properly earned and every penny of profit duly accounted for. It's all laid out in here – wonderfully neat and accurate. I've seen worse accounts presented to me by a professional.'

Ellie-Mae blushed, but looked rather pleased.

'And I don't know if you've all seen the website that Ned built.' Uncle Rufus looked round the room again. 'But if you haven't, you should. It's simple to use, fun to look at, fast to load, and if you're wondering why this business took off in the way it did, that website is a large part of the reason!'

Ned looked rather pleased with himself as well.

'And as for your card designs, young lady . . .' Uncle Rufus had turned to Mo. 'What can I say? The basis of any business is a good product and your drawings are exactly that – funny, witty, clever – they are simply first class!'

Mo blushed, and her mother leaned forward and patted her on the shoulder.

'And then we have Felix here' – Uncle Rufus gestured to his nephew – 'who's seen how good the cards are, gets the idea that maybe he can sell a few, pulls in his friends to help and . . .' He looked around the table. 'I'll tell you now, if I had a son who'd done all that – who'd done what any of you have done – I would be so proud. *So* proud!'

The atmosphere in the room, Felix noticed, had changed while his uncle had been talking. Somehow, the feeling of tension had gone, and the adults were all smiling now as they murmured their agreement.

'But the thing is,' Uncle Rufus was talking again, 'that success on this level means the business will need to have a slightly more formal organization. I gather that, previously, the profits have been shared out every few weeks on Felix's bedroom floor – and that was fine when only small amounts of money were involved. But the sums are larger now, and I would suggest that means that a proper partnership agreement is required.' He looked carefully round the room. 'So we'll need to know what *sort* of partnership is wanted, and the only people who can answer that question, of course, are the partners themselves. But with the rest of us keeping an eye on what they do, to make sure that whatever they decide is fair to everyone.'

He paused for a moment and looked in turn at each of the four children.

'It's the sort of thing that can sometimes get a bit complicated, so I've got a little exercise that might help.'

He reached forward to the shoebox in the middle of the table, lifted the lid of the box, and carefully took out six ten-pound notes, four five-pound notes and twenty one-pound coins.

'We'll start with you, I think, Felix.' Uncle Rufus pushed the money across the table towards his nephew. 'You've got a hundred pounds there. I want you to imagine it's the profit from your business, and I want you to share it between yourself and your three partners. You can share it any way you like. You might think that, because the business was your idea, you should have most of the money. Or you might think that Mo here should have most of it, because she designed the cards. Or maybe Ned should have the biggest share because his website was so successful, or perhaps you think Ellie-Mae's work on the accounts is worth a bit extra . . . You just share it out in the way you think would be best.'

He looked round at other three. 'And while he's doing it, you can all be thinking about what *you* think would be fair, because very shortly I'm going to be asking you the same question.'

Felix barely hesitated before dividing the money in front of him into four equal piles.

'Twenty-five pounds for each of you?' said his uncle. 'You think that would be the fairest division of the partnership and any money it makes?'

'It's what we've been doing so far,' said Felix. 'And if everyone has an equal share, it means nobody's going to think they're being cheated.'

'OK.' Uncle Rufus swept up all the money into a single pile again and pushed it over towards Mo. 'What about you, Mo? How would you share out the hundred pounds?'

'Well, I don't think it should be equal shares,' said Mo. 'Felix is the one that made all this happen, and he does most of the work. It was his idea. He prints all the cards and sends them out. He's the one who got Ned to do a website and Ellie-Mae to do the accounts. None of this would have happened without him. I think he should have . . . half.'

She took out fifty pounds and pushed it towards Felix. 'And I think the rest of us should share out the other fifty between us.'

She tried sharing out the money but found dividing fifty pounds into three equal parts was not easy.

'Don't worry about it . . .' Uncle Rufus made a note on his jotter. 'You think fifty per cent for Felix and the rest to be divided between the three of you . . . OK.' He gathered up the money again and pushed it down the table. 'Your turn, Ned.'

Ned considered the matter carefully before he spoke. 'I think Mo's right that Felix should get most because he's done the most work,' he said, eventually. 'But I think Mo should have almost as much because she's the one who designed the cards. I know my website's good, but Felix told me what to write and it only took me a few week-ends and compared to those two . . .' He started pushing the money into piles. 'I think, if I was sharing out the hundred pounds, I'd give forty pounds to Felix, thirty pounds to Mo, and fifteen each to me and Ellie-Mae.'

'Well, we're getting some very interesting answers here,' said Uncle Rufus, as he wrote down Ned's sugges-tion. 'Thank you, Ned. If you could pass the money over to Ellie-Mae, please?'

Ned was about to sweep up the money into one pile and push it across, when Ellie-Mae reached out a hand and stopped him.

Without speaking, she took a fiver from her own pile and put it on Felix's, and then a fiver from Ned's pile and put it on Mo's, then leaned back in her chair.

'You are suggesting,' said Uncle Rufus, 'that it should be forty-five per cent for Felix, thirty-five per cent for Mo and ten per cent each for yourself and Ned . . . is that right?'

Ellie-Mae nodded.

'OK . . .' Uncle Rufus made a note of this on his pad and turned back to Felix.

'The others all seem to think you should have the biggest share – certainly more than a quarter. Would you be prepared to go along with that?'

'Yes, of course,' said Felix. 'I just didn't want there to be any . . . you know . . .'

'Quite.' Uncle Rufus turned to Mo. 'And what about you, Mo? They seem to think you should have a bit more as well. Is that all right with you?'

'I could probably cope,' said Mo.

'So, it seems the only real point of disagreement we have is whether Ellie-Mae and Ned should have ten or fifteen per cent each,' said Uncle Rufus, 'and I'm going to step in here and suggest we split the difference. Let's give each of you twelve and a half per cent. Which means that, in future, whenever the business makes a profit of a hundred pounds, Felix here will have £42.50, Mo will have £32.50, and you two will have £12.50. Do we think that's a fair way of sharing things out between the four of you?'

All four children nodded.

'OK.' Uncle Rufus looked round the room. 'I don't know how the rest of you feel, but I think our four partners here have come up with a very reasonable division of the profits based on what they have each contributed. Felix gets most because the business was his idea and he's done most of the work. Mo gets the next largest share because she designed the cards, and for the vital and superbly performed tasks of computer support and accounting, Ellie-Mae and Ned get twelve and a half per cent each.'

He looked round at the parents. 'What about the rest of you? Does anyone feel their child has been hard done by and deserves more?'

There was a general shaking of heads and a murmur that, yes, the division seemed very fair.

'Shall we vote on it then?' Uncle Rufus picked up his pen. 'All those in favour of setting up a business partnership between these four along the lines we've just outlined, please raise your hand.'

Everyone in the room raised their hand.

'Unanimous!' Uncle Rufus smiled approvingly. 'That's the way we like it!' He picked up his clipboard from the table.

'Right,' he said. 'Item two . . .'

Felix stared at his uncle in astonishment, hardly able to believe what had happened. He had not expected his uncle to raise the subject of sharing out the money at all and, when he did, he had certainly not expected that it would be settled the way it had – in barely ten minutes, with nobody arguing, with everybody apparently quite happy, and with Felix himself getting the largest share of the cash.

For the life of him, Felix couldn't work out how his uncle had done it.

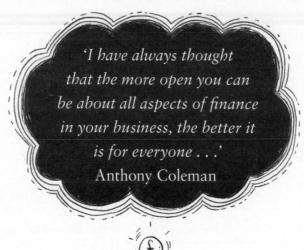

'I have always thought
that the more open you can
be about all aspects of finance
in your business, the better it
is for everyone ...'
Anthony Coleman

## CHAPTER TWELVE

# Paying Dividends

'Item two on the agenda,' said Uncle Rufus, 'is sharing out the money we have in that box there. According to Ellie-Mae's excellent accounts, we know that it contains £4,319.65. We've decided *how* that money is going to be shared out, so the next decision is – do we want to share it now? Do we want to do it later? Do we want to share out *all* of it, or just some of it? In which case, how much?' He turned to Felix. 'Let's start with you again, Felix. What do you think?'

'We'll need to keep some in the box,' said Felix, 'so I can buy stamps and envelopes and paper. And a new printer. That's going to cost a bit.'

'How about we share out half,' suggested Mo, 'and keep half in reserve?'

'If we shared out three thousand pounds,' said Ned, 'you'd still have over a thousand in reserve. That ought to be enough, shouldn't it, to buy whatever we need?'

Felix agreed that it would probably be enough. More than enough really.

Uncle Rufus turned to Ellie-Mae. 'How much would everyone get if we shared out three thousand pounds among the partnership?' he asked.

Ellie-Mae answered without hesitating.

'Ned and I would get £375 each,' she said. 'Mo would get £975 and Felix would get £1,275.'

'OK . . .' Uncle Rufus looked around the room. 'The proposal is that the partnership pay out a dividend of three thousand pounds to be shared in the proportions that the partnership has already agreed. All those in favour?'

Everyone in the room put their hand up.

'My word, we are doing well!' Uncle Rufus smiled, and pushed the box of money towards Ellie-Mae. 'I think dishing out the cash is a job for our accountant, and while she's doing it, perhaps the rest of us could put our minds to item three.'

He tapped the table with his pen before continuing.

'Felix tells me that, as of lunchtime today, he has

orders for a hundred and fourteen sets of cards which he cannot fill because the printer's broken, and the shop that usually sells him padded envelopes doesn't have any in stock. Ned's website promises that cards will be sent out within a day of being ordered, and I think this is one of those occasions where the rest of us have to step in and do what we can to help.'

He glanced round the room, but this time looking at the adults, rather than the children.

'What our four partners need is for there to be a hundred and fourteen sets of cards, in their envelopes, addressed, stamped and ready to be posted, on this table before the day ends. Any suggestions how we do that?'

What followed seemed to happen with remarkable speed. In a matter of minutes Felix's father had gone off to buy a new printer – Uncle Rufus suggested as he left, that he might as well get two while he was at it – while Felix explained to everyone about addressing the bags, what had to go in each of them, and how a record of each order needed to be written down in the exercise book.

Mo's mother offered to do the run to Southampton to find somewhere that sold padded envelopes. Ellie-Mae's grandmother went out to buy three hundred stamps from the local post office, while Ned and his father went into town to get what he called a 'proper supply' of card, and ordinary envelopes – they came back with enough to keep the business going for a month. Ellie-Mae sat at the dining-room table with the shoebox of money, giving out cash to people when they needed to buy something, collecting the receipts when they came back, and writing everything down in the accounts book. Felix's mother and his brother William, meanwhile, started packing up and addressing what padded envelopes they already had.

Half an hour later, Felix's father was back and unpacking the first of the printers, and soon after that there was what looked like a factory style production line set up on the dining-room table. Felix's father printed the cards, Mo and her mother folded them and packed them, with their envelopes, into cellophane bags, and William and Felix's mother had the job of writing the addresses on the padded envelopes. Ellie-Mae's grandmother put on the stamps, Ned checked that each envelope was packed with everything that was needed before sealing them up, while Ellie-Mae wrote down the details of each order in the exercise book.

The only people who didn't seem to have a job in all this were Felix and Uncle Rufus.

'I ought to be doing something, shouldn't I?' said Felix. 'I can't just stand here and watch.'

'Your job,' said his uncle, 'is to come out in the garden with me, so we can sort out item four.'

Item four on Uncle Rufus's list was working out how Felix was going to keep up with printing and sending out the cards if the orders kept coming in at the same rate once half term was over and he had gone back to school.

Sitting in the garden, his uncle made Felix go through all the things that had to be done to make sure forty or fifty packs of cards were sent out to the right people, and Felix told him that, if the orders continued at the present rate, it would probably take at least four hours each day.

'There's no way you're going to do that on your own, is there?' said Uncle Rufus. 'You'll need to find someone who can do most of it for you.'

Felix agreed. He had been thinking about people he knew at school, and there were several who could probably do the work, but none of them had any more free time than he did himself.

'What about your brother?' said Uncle Rufus, looking back towards the house, where William could be seen at the dining-room table, addressing the padded envelopes. 'I heard he's out of a job at the moment. Is he reliable?'

'Reliable' was in fact precisely the word people usually used to describe Felix's brother. His school reports had often said how 'solid' and 'dependable' he was. They didn't use words like 'clever', or 'bright', or 'imaginative', but all his teachers had always agreed that William was . . . 'reliable'.

'He'd be perfect,' said Felix, though he couldn't help thinking there was something a little strange about employing his own brother, particularly one who was six years older than himself. 'But . . . I don't know if he'd want to do it.'

'Let's go and ask him, shall we?' said Uncle Rufus.

'Can I ask you something first?' said Felix.

'What?'

'I've been wondering why . . . in there' – Felix pointed towards the house – 'Ned and Ellie-Mae agreed to have a smaller share of the money.'

Uncle Rufus gave a little shrug. 'They were asked what they thought was fair and that's what they came up with. I think they got it about right, don't you?'

'Maybe,' said Felix, 'but it is a lot less money.'

'It is,' Uncle Rufus agreed, 'but remember when I told you a first rule of business was when you don't know how to do something, find someone who does? Well, some skills are easier to find than others, and I think your friends were smart enough to know that. Smart enough to realize that the work they did could be done by plenty of others, while you'd have to look a long way to find another Mo. Or someone to replace you, for that matter. Like I said, I thought they got it about right. And money-wise, they're not doing too badly.' He stood up. 'Come on, let's go and talk to your brother.'

It turned out that William was more than happy to take the job, though he did want to know how much he would be paid.

Felix looked at his uncle.

'How about the same as you were getting at the tea factory?' asked Uncle Rufus. 'Two pounds an hour over the minimum wage, right?'

Felix had no idea how much this was, but William brightened considerably at the prospect.

'Great!' he said. 'When do I start?'

'It looks to me like you already have,' said Uncle Rufus. 'Keep a track of how many hours you do today, and then have a talk with Felix at some point to make sure you know what he needs you to do in future.'

'OK,' said William, and he headed back to the dining room looking more cheerful than Felix had seen him in days.

Soon after four, a little over two hours after his uncle had sat down to start the meeting, the dining-room table was stacked with a hundred and fourteen padded envelopes, each neatly addressed, each containing a set of ten cards, and all stamped and ready for William to take down to the post. Not only that, there was a further stack of two thousand cards – two hundred of each design – printed and folded, ready for any orders that might come in during the next few days. And while everyone was admiring the result of their labours, and looking rather pleased with themselves . . . the pizza arrived.

The pizza was Uncle Rufus's idea, though Felix was the one who paid for it.

'It's what managers do,' his uncle had told him, 'whenever they've asked people to make a special effort or work overtime for some reason. It's a way of showing you appreciate what was done. And it's a more important part of the job than you might think.'

They moved out to the garden to eat, and Felix's parents produced some cans of cola and mugs of tea, and people sat around and talked. They talked mostly about the business of course – how it had started, all the decisions that had been taken along the way – and looking around at them, Felix couldn't help thinking how different it all was from how he had imagined it would be. All his worries about losing control over the business, of having to do what other people told him to do instead of what he wanted, had all vanished. If anything, he seemed to have *more* control of things than he had before, and certainly a lot less to worry about. A system had been set up to look after the next orders, a new agreement made on how to share out the money . . . And the extraordinary thing was that it had all been sorted in a couple of hours, without anyone getting upset, and without even the hint of an argument.

Felix still wasn't quite sure *how* it had happened, but he did know who was responsible.

His uncle, thought Felix, was a genius, and he went across to try and say thank you.

'Seemed to go all right, didn't it?' Uncle Rufus looked around the garden and then back at Felix. 'Don't forget you owe me £12.75,' he said.

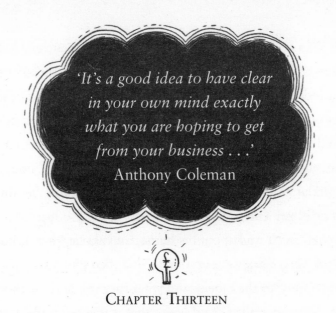

'It's a good idea to have clear in your own mind exactly what you are hoping to get from your business . . .'
Anthony Coleman

CHAPTER THIRTEEN

# The Partnership

On Monday, when Felix walked into school with Mo, they found Ned and Ellie-Mae waiting for them at the gates, eager to talk about everything that had happened over the weekend.

'Did you see the look on my dad's face when your uncle told everyone how much profit we'd made?' Ned said happily. 'In the car when we were driving over, he was muttering that he'd warned me never to let myself get dragged into another of "Felix's wild ideas". And on the way back he kept telling me how clever I'd been and how, if I ever wanted any help with programming the website, I only had to ask!'

Mo had already reported a similar experience with her mother, and Ellie-Mae said she had overheard her grandmother boasting to a friend about a business that 'her granddaughter had set up with some classmates', and telling them to go online and order some cards for themselves.

The talking continued through break and on into lunchtime. The others particularly wanted to hear about Felix's uncle and about his house, and about what he had said when Felix went up there – and then the talk turned, inevitably, to the money and what they might do with it.

'Do you realize,' said Ned, 'that if it goes on like this, we could be getting like . . . thousands of pounds a year?'

'Do you think it *will* go on like this?' Ellie-Mae asked Felix.

'I don't know,' he told her.

'I hope it does,' said Mo. 'There's a lot you can buy with a few thousand pounds.'

Her own dream was to be able to walk into the art shop in the High Street and pick out anything and every-thing she wanted – all the pens, the coloured inks, the paints and the papers – without even thinking about how much it would cost, and whether or not she could afford it.

Ned was planning to spend most of his share of the

profits on computer games, and possibly one of the new games consoles that had recently appeared on the market.

Ellie-Mae, when Mo asked, said she was hoping to save up enough to buy a cello of her own, instead of using the one that she borrowed from the school. She had been talking about it with her music teacher and it seemed that, for a few thousand, she could purchase something quite decent.

'And what about you, Felix?' she asked. 'What will you do with your share?'

'I don't know,' Felix told her. 'I haven't really thought about it.'

And it was true. He had given very little consideration to how he might spend the money he had made. It was setting up the business and managing it that was the interesting bit. What he might do with the money once he had made it was, at the moment at least, somehow much less important.

The one thing they didn't talk about, and Felix felt reluctant to bring up the subject himself, was the new way of sharing out the profits that had been agreed at the meeting on Saturday. Despite his uncle's reassurances and the fact that Ned and Ellie-Mae had actually suggested the new arrangement themselves, Felix couldn't help wondering if perhaps they regretted it now, and were silently wishing they could go back to everyone having equal shares.

He asked Mo about it, as they were walking home together. She had always been good at knowing what other people were thinking or feeling, even when they hadn't actually said anything, and he knew she could probably tell him if either Ned or Ellie-Mae were having second thoughts about the way the profits were now divided.

'Because they're only getting half what they would have got if we were still sharing it equally,' he said. 'It's all right for you and me, we're getting more than before, but . . . you think they really don't mind?'

'Ellie-Mae told me she prefers it the way it is now,' said Mo.

'She *prefers* getting less money?'

Mo nodded. 'She said it didn't feel right before. Like she was cheating somehow. She knew you were doing hours of work every day, and it was you set it all up, and it was you who had all the ideas about what to do next – while she did a half hour of maths each week and got the same money. She said it didn't matter too much at first, but when the numbers got so much bigger it felt . . . wrong. So when your uncle asked what she thought would be fair, she could tell him, and she says it feels much better now.'

'And Ned?'

'Ned said that, for the money he's already had, you could have hired a professional to do what he did, and not given him a share at all. He's very happy to get what he's getting.'

Felix was reassured by this, and equally reassured when he got home to find sixty-two padded envelopes sitting on the dining-room table, all neatly addressed, packed and stamped, and with the details carefully recorded in the columns of the exercise book.

'I haven't sealed them up yet,' William told him, 'in case you want to check they're OK, but if they are, I'll stick them down and take them off to the post.'

'I'm sure they're fine,' said Felix. 'You go ahead.'

On Sunday he had, as his uncle suggested, gone through the process of filling the orders with William, and quickly discovered that his brother was as careful and reliable in the way he worked as everyone said he was. Not particularly fast, but . . . reliable.

'I've done the money as well. I hope that's all right.' William pointed to a pile of neatly opened brown envelopes and a wodge of money at the far end of the table. 'There were eighty-one of them. I've ticked them all off in the book.'

'Eighty-one?' Felix picked up the pile of ten-pound notes. 'I like the sound of that.'

'Yes.' William paused a moment in the business of sealing up the envelopes and looked across at his brother 'You're lucky, aren't you?'

'Getting this much money in one day?' Felix was staring at the banknotes in his hand. 'Yes. I think I am.'

'I wasn't talking about the money,' said William. 'I meant . . . this is what you've always wanted, isn't it? You wanted to set up a proper business, and now you have. You're doing what you always wanted. That's why I said you were lucky.'

Later, sitting on his bedroom floor, still holding eighty-one ten-pound notes, Felix found himself thinking about that. It *was* good to have the money but this wasn't, as he had told the others at school, because there was anything in particular he wanted to buy. The satisfaction came rather from the extraordinary realization that he had somehow set up a business that meant he came home from school on an ordinary Monday to find £810 waiting for him in brown envelopes delivered by the postman. That was the part that was *really* satisfying.

And his brother was right. He was lucky.

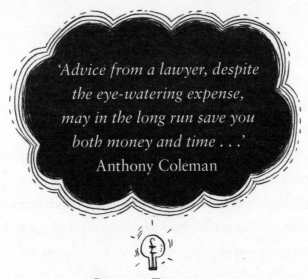

*'Advice from a lawyer, despite the eye-watering expense, may in the long run save you both money and time . . .'*
Anthony Coleman

## CHAPTER FOURTEEN

# Signing the Deal

Three days later, shortly after Felix had got back from school, he answered the door to find his uncle standing on the step.

'A little something for you to think about,' he said, holding out a large manila envelope. 'I can leave it with you or, if you've got a moment, I could come in and explain.'

Felix invited him into the living room, where his uncle reached into the envelope and took out several closely typed pages that had been stapled together.

'It's a draft proposal for a partnership agreement,' he

said, passing it to Felix. 'There are copies for the others as well, and a letter explaining what you all need to do next.'

Felix took his copy of the agreement and glanced at the opening paragraphs.

'It may not make much sense to you,' said his uncle. 'Lawyers seem to have a language all their own. But I think you'd be wise to put the business on a proper legal footing. So show it to your parents, will you? Then make sure the others do the same, and let me know what you all think.

'As it says in my letter,' he went on, 'it is only a suggestion. If there's anything in it you don't like, or that you want to change, or if you don't want to have a formal agreement at all, you only have to say. It's your business. I'm just here to offer advice.'

'I'm sure this is brilliant . . .' Felix was riffling through the pages. 'But isn't it going to be kind of expensive?'

'A lawyer friend ran it up for me,' said his uncle. 'Didn't take him long, and it's pretty standard stuff. Think of it as an early birthday present.'

It was, Felix suspected, an extremely generous birthday present and he was still in the process of trying to say thank you when his brother appeared from the kitchen.

'I thought I heard someone,' he said. 'Cup of tea, Uncle?'

'Next time perhaps,' said Uncle Rufus. 'I'm a bit rushed today. How's the new job going?'

'Not too bad,' William told him. 'Boss can be a bit of a pain sometimes, but the money's OK, and getting to work is really easy!'

'That sounds good!' Uncle Rufus smiled, then turned back to Felix. 'Perhaps you could organize another partnership meeting for, say, three weeks' time? I can do the Saturday, if that works for everyone else.'

The partnership meeting three weeks later was chaired, at Felix's request, by Uncle Rufus, who began by apologizing for the fact that a lot of what he was going to say would probably sound quite boring, but he hoped everyone would try and stay awake, because it was important. He promised that, with a bit of luck, it wouldn't take longer than an hour.

The partnership agreement, as he went through it line by line, laid out exactly what the partnership was for, how the profits were to be divided up, exactly what each of the partners promised to do, how often they should meet, who had the right to call a meeting, and who should be in charge of it when they did. It said how voting at the meetings should be conducted, how the records of each meeting should be kept and who should have them. It said how the accounts of how much money had been made and what it had been spent on should be kept, and also how they should be made available to any of the partners or their guardians, who wanted to see them.

The agreement also laid out what should happen if someone wanted to change the terms of the partnership, or if one of the partners fell ill, or if they died, or if they decided they didn't want to be a partner any more. It said what should happen to their share of the business in those circumstances, who they could sell their share to and how the value of that share should be worked out.

At the end – and it was almost exactly an hour before Uncle Rufus was finished – he asked if there were any questions and, ten minutes later, called for a vote on whether everyone approved the terms of the partnership or whether anyone wanted more time to think about it all.

The vote to sign was unanimous and, because there was a copy for each of the partners, they all had to sign all of them, and each copy was passed round the table and each of the guardians signed as well as Felix, Mo, Ned and Ellie-Mae. It was, Felix thought, a bit like a picture he had once seen of people signing an international treaty.

And once that was all done, Ellie-Mae gave everyone copies she had printed out of the figures for the profits Kardmart had made since the last partnership meeting. It was a little under £7,000, after all expenses, including William's wages, had been paid, and another vote was taken on how much should be shared out. They decided to keep a reserve of one thousand pounds, and Ellie-Mae solemnly passed out thick rolls of banknotes while recording the amounts carefully in a notebook.

It was, one way and another, a cheery occasion and there was a lot of smiling and laughing as people left to go home.

Uncle Rufus, when Felix gave him his consultant's fee – £25.05 – thanked him, placed the money carefully in his pocket and was about to leave when Mrs Farmer came over and asked if he'd like to stay for supper.

'William's done a roast,' she said. 'But if you need to get back to Ludmila, we'll quite understand.'

'As a matter of fact she's away at the moment,' said Uncle Rufus. 'Visiting her family in Poprad.'

'William does a brilliant roast,' said Felix. 'You should definitely stay!'

Uncle Rufus hesitated briefly, but then seemed to relax. 'Thank you,' he said. 'In that case, I will.'

William was in charge of the evening meal every Saturday, and he was an excellent cook, but it was not the food that Felix remembered afterwards about that evening. There are some occasions that seem special, not because of anything in particular that is eaten, or even what is said, but because of how they feel. And the mood that evening was for some reason especially warm and welcoming.

Uncle Rufus was a visitor that everyone seemed particularly glad to see, and it was equally clear that he was glad to be there. The conversation mostly involved remembering a lot of stories about the past – Felix particularly enjoyed the ones about his uncle's first attempts to make money when he was younger – and with all the talk, the meal went on much longer than usual. It was already late when Felix's father appeared with a pot of coffee and the remains of Felix's birthday cake in case anyone was still hungry.

The birthday cake, also made by William, had been moulded in the shape of a Ferrari, and there was still enough of it left to recognize the fact.

'Why a Ferrari?' asked Uncle Rufus.

'Because Felix is going to own a Ferrari one day,'

said Mr Farmer with a smile. 'He told us when he was four.'

'Really?' Uncle Rufus looked across at Felix, who gave a shrug.

'I was waiting with the boys at the bus stop one afternoon,' Mrs Farmer explained, 'trying to get home after a shopping trip. The rain was pouring down, the bus was late, we were all rather tired – and this man drove up in a Ferrari and asked if anyone wanted a lift.'

'Unfortunately, he wasn't talking to us,' said William, taking up the story. 'He was talking to this group of girls in front of us, and two of them got in and he drove off.'

'And Felix said, why can't we have a car like that?' This was Mrs Farmer again. 'I told him we didn't have enough money, but then he wanted to know why the man had enough money, but we didn't. And one of the girls in front turned round and said it was because he was a successful businessman.'

'And Felix thought about it for a bit,' said William, 'and then said in this loud voice, *One day I'm going to be a businessman . . .*'

'*. . . And I'm going to buy a Ferrari!*'

It was one of those family stories that get told so often that everyone knows the last line and laughs as they say it together.

'A Ferrari, eh?' Uncle Rufus smiled across the table at Felix. 'Not a bad choice.'

'We've always thought it was a bit of joke,' said Mrs Farmer, 'but these last few weeks I'm beginning to wonder.'

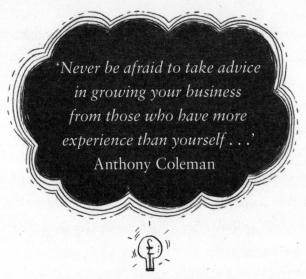

*'Never be afraid to take advice in growing your business from those who have more experience than yourself . . .'*
Anthony Coleman

## CHAPTER FIFTEEN

# Consulting the Consultant

The time that followed was a particularly happy one for Felix. For a start, his business continued to make a great deal of money. At the partnership meeting at the end of June, Ellie-Mae reported that they had sold 10,740 cards that month and it was decided to share out a further £7,500 of the profits between the partners. Felix's share was £3,187.50.

It was an astonishing sum, and equally astonishing, as Ned said, was that the money came in with almost no effort from the partners themselves. Now that William was in charge of printing the cards, checking the orders and sending them out, there was very little even for Felix to do when he got home from school each day. Usually, he just listened while William told him how well they had done, and then took the money upstairs and put it in the shoebox under his bed.

Sometimes, if William was still addressing envelopes when Felix got home, he would join in and help finish off, but this was only because he enjoyed doing it. William was happy to look after all the day-to-day work, including all the shopping for card and envelopes and stamps.

The fact that Kardmart was flourishing, however, was not the only thing contributing to Felix's happiness. Every bit as important, if not more so, was the relationship with his newly discovered uncle.

After that second partnership meeting, Uncle Rufus had taken to calling in at the house at least once a week to see how things were going. His car would draw up at the pavement sometime in the late afternoon soon after Felix had got back from school. Uncle Rufus would explain that he was on his way to or from some meeting or other and ask if it was a convenient time to talk. Then Felix would make a pot of tea and the two of them would sit in the kitchen or the front room and Felix would tell him how Kardmart was doing and ask his uncle's advice about anything that was bothering him.

And the thing about advice from Uncle Rufus was that it was exactly that – advice. He never *told* Felix what to do. The business, he always said, belonged to Felix and his partners, and they were the ones in charge of making all the decisions regarding its future.

So when Uncle Rufus suggested, for instance, that the partnership should open a bank account, rather than keep its money in a shoebox under the bed, Felix thought about it, but decided he preferred things as they were. He explained that he liked being able to actually *see* the money that he was making, and he liked the way that, when it came to sharing it out, Ellie-Mae would reach into the box and take out the rolls of notes and pass them round. It was, for him, all part of the fun. And Uncle Rufus simply smiled and nodded, and did not mention the subject again.

It was his father who persuaded Felix to change his mind on that one. He pointed out at supper one evening the difficulties that would follow if, for any reason, the money went missing. Or if there was a fire. Or a burglary. Who would be responsible? he asked. Would Felix have to pay the others back out of his own share? Was it really worth taking the risk?

After much thought, and after discussing it with Mo and the others, Felix had accepted that a bank account would, after all, be the sensible option. Two days later his uncle Rufus took all four of them down to a bank in the High Street where a cheerful young woman explained how a partnership account worked, how to set it up, and then helped each of them open individual accounts at the same time.

If she was surprised at being given an old shoebox containing several thousand pounds as the first deposit, she did her best not to show it.

And Uncle Rufus did more than simply give advice. In an emergency he gave practical help as well. There was, for instance, the time Felix got back from school to find a horrified William standing by the computer, pointing to the screen which was blank, apart from one line which said there was an error.

'Something's happened,' he said. 'I can't get it to do anything!'

'Why? What's wrong?'

'I don't know! One minute it was fine and then . . . it says there's this error.'

The only remedy Felix knew to a computer problem was the one Ned had told him, about pulling out the plug and then putting it back in again. William said he had tried that four times and it hadn't worked.

The first thing Felix would normally have done was call Ned, but Ned was in California, officially on a course to learn about computer programming and, judging from his postcards, also having an early summer holiday.

One possible solution would be to go out and buy a new computer but, Felix thought, that would still leave the problem of what would happen to that day's orders in the meantime. And what would happen to all the names and addresses of people who had bought cards in the past? Was all that information going to be lost as well?

Felix rang his uncle.

Thirty minutes later, a young man in a white van drew up outside the house, and an hour after that the computer was running again. The man also provided an external hard drive and gave both Felix and William a long lecture on the importance of backing everything up at least once a day, and preferably every hour.

When Felix asked how much he owed him, the young man charged for the cost of the hard drive, but refused to take anything for either his time or his labour.

'Your uncle was a big help to me when I was setting up,' he said. 'It's nice to have a chance to do something for him in return.' He passed over a business card. 'But if you're ever thinking of buying a new machine, give me a call. I can do you a very competitive price!'

*

But the best thing about Uncle Rufus, better even than the advice he gave or the help he could provide, was simply being able to talk to him about . . . business.

Sitting in the kitchen with a mug of tea in his hand, his uncle would talk, not just about Kardmart, but about what he called 'the game'. Setting up a business, he often said, was the best game in the world. But like all games, it had its rules and, if you wanted to play successfully, it was important to learn what they were. They were rules like the one he had told Felix that first day he had been brought out to the house – *When you don't know how to do something, find someone who does.*

And perhaps the most important rule, he said, and the thing that most people didn't understand about the game, was that it never stood still. A business was not something you could simply set up and leave to run. You had to be constantly changing, updating and reinventing it. If your business wasn't growing, he would say, then it was almost certainly dying.

He would talk about the business he was involved in at the time – he had recently become the major UK supplier of batteries for forklift trucks – and about others he had set up in the past. He would tell stories of the mistakes he had made – of ventures that had gone spectacularly wrong, and others that went unexpectedly right – and how he had learned from experiencing both.

He could explain all the phrases that Felix had come across in books like the one by Anthony Coleman, and hadn't properly understood – like *cash flow*, or *cornering a market*, or what a *gross margin* was. It even turned out that his uncle had not only read the book by Anthony Coleman that Mo had given Felix, but had actually met the man on several occasions.

'First time I heard him speak was at a conference for small businesses in Birmingham,' said Uncle Rufus. 'He'd just set up the first twenty-four-hour plumbing business in Britain and made a lot of money. I liked him. He's a good man.'

Being with Uncle Rufus was like being with no one else that Felix had ever met. He talked about all the things that Felix had always wanted to talk about. He knew about all the things that Felix wanted to know about, and he seemed to have done all the things that Felix wanted one day to do himself.

His uncle Rufus was, Felix thought . . . brilliant.

Absolutely brilliant.

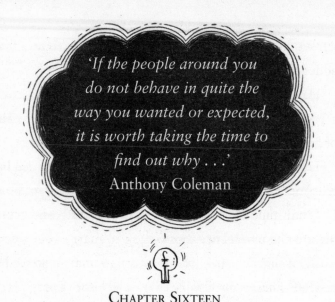

CHAPTER SIXTEEN

# Business Background

'The thing I don't understand,' Felix told Mo as they were walking back together from school one afternoon towards the end of the summer term, 'is why I had to wait till I was nearly thirteen before I even met him. I mean, he only lives eight miles away, and he's the one person who would have been really useful to know! Why didn't Mum or Dad let me meet him earlier?'

'Well, they *wanted* you to meet him,' said Mo. 'I mean, they kept inviting him to the house and things, didn't they? But he refused.'

Felix stared at her. 'What?'

'Wouldn't even reply, would he?' Mo paused and then added thoughtfully, 'I suppose he was still angry.'

'Angry? What about?'

'Well . . . about your mum marrying your dad instead of him.'

Felix came to an abrupt halt in the middle of a zebra crossing. '*What?*'

'Your mum' – Mo took Felix's arm and led him gently over to the pavement – 'was going to marry your uncle, wasn't she? But then she decided to marry your dad instead. That's why they hadn't spoken for twenty years, isn't it?' She paused again. 'You didn't know?'

'No,' said Felix. 'Nobody told me.'

'Oh, sorry.' Mo smiled apologetically. 'I thought everyone knew.'


When Felix got home, as he let himself in the front door, he heard his brother's voice call from the dining room.

'Thirty-two today!'

William always greeted Felix with the news of how many orders they had received that day.

Felix left his bag in the hall and went into the dining room. On the table was a pile of padded envelopes, filled and ready to be taken down to the post. There was another pile of brown envelopes that had been opened and the money inside them was neatly stacked ready for Felix to check before William took it down to bank, and the order book was open so he could see all the details freshly filled in.

'And Rufus's idea worked,' said William. 'Four of the non-payers have coughed up!'

As Anthony Coleman had warned, not everyone who received their cards remembered to pay for them, and Uncle Rufus had suggested that in some cases this might simply be a matter of forgetfulness, and that a reminder might help. Felix had worked out a letter to send to them after waiting a month, which said:

*I hope you liked the cards we sent. Unfortunately we haven't received any money for them yet. If you've already sent it, please ignore this; if not, we are enclosing another stamped addressed envelope.*

If they still didn't reply, Uncle Rufus said, it was probably best to write off the loss and forget about it. Apparently, in four cases, the reminder had worked.

'Did you know,' asked Felix, 'about Mum and Uncle Rufus?'

'What about them?'

'That they nearly got married.'

'Oh, that!' William chuckled. 'Yes.'

'You did?'

'I think Gran told me the story one day.' William gestured to a box of stationery. 'We're going to need more card by the way. Shall I pick it up when I take this lot down to the post?'

'Yes, thank you . . .' Felix was not really listening. 'Is Mum in yet?'

'In the kitchen,' said William. 'It's Thursday.'

William had taken over most of the cooking for the family. He had always done the Saturday roast and been in charge of making cakes and puddings, but now, as he was the one with the most spare hours even after his work for Kardmart, he had suggested he be in charge of preparing the evening meal each day, as an alternative to paying rent.

It was an arrangement that suited everyone, but Felix's mother said she didn't want to be completely shut out of her own kitchen, and one day a week she came home early from work to take over making the evening meal herself.

Felix found her standing at the sink, peeling some potatoes for a cottage pie. She gave him a smile and gestured to a plate on the table.

'Your brother's made some meringues,' she said. 'You should try one. They're good.'

'Is it true,' Felix asked, 'that you were going to marry Uncle Rufus, but changed your mind?'

'Goodness!' His mother gave an odd laugh and a pink flush rose to her cheeks. 'Who have you been talking to?'

'Mo,' said Felix. 'Is it true?'

'Well . . . yes. I suppose it is.' His mother had turned back to the sink and was scraping vigorously at a potato. 'Though strictly speaking, your uncle was the one who changed his mind. A week before the wedding. He disappeared off to France, leaving a letter saying he needed to think about things. Then six months later he came back and said he'd decided he *did* want to marry me after all. But by that time I'd decided to marry your father instead.'

'You were engaged to *both* of them?'

'Not at the same time!' Mrs Farmer cut the peeled potato into sections before putting it in a saucepan. 'It was . . . complicated. Uncle Rufus and your father were very different, and I liked them both. Most people did. Rufus was the one with the money who could take you out to fancy restaurants, of course. Your father's idea of taking a girl on a date was a walk in the woods in the rain.' She threw some salt in with the potatoes. 'But it turned out he was the one I wanted.'

'Why didn't anyone tell me about all this before?' demanded Felix.

'I did try,' said his mother. 'A couple of times. But you didn't seem very interested. So I stopped.' She turned up the heat under the saucepan. 'Anyway, Rufus was very upset when I told him. Refused to come to the wedding, and basically never spoke to us again. We kept hoping he'd get over it. We invited him for Christmas, asked him to be William's godparent and things, but . . . he was very angry. He wouldn't have anything to do with us.'

Felix stared at her, and the memory flashed into his mind of that first visit to his uncle's house. How his father had not been invited inside, and how neither of the two brothers had even reached out to shake hands. And then, when he left, he had found his mother waiting outside for him as well, and there was that hug that she had given Uncle Rufus, and the odd way that he had resisted at first and then . . .

'You know . . .' Mrs Farmer was gazing out the window down the garden as she spoke. 'A lot of good things have happened as a result of you setting up your business. Apart from it being a success and making all that money, I mean. You gave William a job at the time he needed it most. And what it's done for Mo is just wonderful, she's like a different girl . . . But the best thing that's happened, the *very* best, is what it did for your father.'

Felix frowned. 'What did it do for Dad?'

'It gave him the perfect reason to go to his brother and ask for help. He could ring Rufus and say, *I've got a twelve-year-old son, and he's set up this business*, which was exactly what Rufus was doing when he was your age, *and he needs help and I don't know what to do. Can you talk to him?* He knew it was the one thing that Rufus couldn't resist.'

'Is that why Dad took me out there?'

'Well, he thought your uncle's advice would probably be useful as well, but . . . yes, that was the main reason. It broke through the barrier, you see. Your dad's very fond of his brother. He missed him. And because of you setting up your business, he's got him back.'

For a while the only sound in the kitchen was of the saucepan bubbling on the stove.

'So how's Kardmart doing these days?' asked Felix's mother. 'New cards coming on all right, are they?'

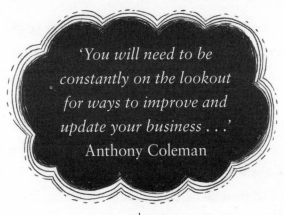

'You will need to be constantly on the lookout for ways to improve and update your business . . .'
Anthony Coleman

CHAPTER SEVENTEEN

# The New Line

Felix had been itching to have more new cards available on the website for some time. He still thought they should be trying to launch a new set of cards every month or so, but the bottleneck was Mo. She had been working on a third set of drawings of 5FW for several weeks now, but without any visible signs of progress. When Felix asked how long it would be before she was finished, she told him she did not know. When he asked if he could see how far she had got, she said no he couldn't. Mo never let anyone see her work while it was 'in progress'.

Felix asked Uncle Rufus if he had any advice to give

on the matter. Was there anything he could be doing, he wondered, to get Mo to speed things up a bit?

'I think you just have to be patient,' his uncle told him, when Felix described the situation. 'You have to be careful with these creative types. If you push too hard, they get all upset and then you don't get anything useful out of them for months. My advice is to sit back and wait.' He paused to take another slice of the banana cake William had provided. 'But if you want a new line of cards, Mo's drawings aren't the only pictures you can use, are they? Aren't there other things you can stick on the front?'

Thinking about it in bed that night, Felix remembered a card he had found in the shop when he had been looking for a birthday card for his mother. It had been a photograph of a man throwing a Frisbee for a tortoise and shouting *Fetch!* It was the sort of picture he could easily have produced himself, he thought, if he had a camera. So maybe if he bought one and . . . and in almost the same instant, he remembered something else, and wondered if he might not even need to do that.

Felix's grandfather had been a professional photographer through the 1950s and 60s, and had left behind a collection of literally thousands of photographs. They were stored in boxes in the spare room at his gran's house, and Felix had spent a good many hours on his visits there looking through them.

Grandfather Jim had had a studio in Southsea and the majority of his photographs were of ordinary people on the beach, or at the funfair, or simply walking down the street. They were mostly in black and white, but they were beautifully sharp and clear, and there was something about the clothes people wore, their hairstyles and the cars they drove, that Felix had found endlessly fascinating. They were like a glimpse of another world.

He called round to his grandmother's house at the weekend, told her he had been wondering if the photos might make interesting cards, and asked if she would mind if he used some of them. Gran said she thought it was a lovely idea, and that her husband would be pleased as punch that his pictures were still being enjoyed, instead of mouldering in boxes.

That afternoon, Felix picked out about twenty pictures that he thought might be suitable and took them into school on Monday to show the others. It was Mo who suggested that they should write something to go below the photos, as she had done with her drawings of 5FW. The four of them spent the lunch-break that day going through the pictures, choosing the ten they liked best, and then thinking up what Mo called the 'caption' that would go underneath.

Ellie-Mae proved particularly good at this. One of the photographs was from the 1950s of a young man standing proudly on the beach in a somewhat baggy pair of swimming trunks. The caption Ellie-Mae came up with was:

*Nothing gave a man more confidence, thought Ralph, than a bathing costume knitted by your mother.*

Another photo, from the same period, was of a smart young couple in a sports car. The man was smoking a pipe, while the girl looked across at him adoringly.

*Felicity wondered*, ran Ellie-Mae's caption, *if now was a good time to tell Sebastian she had just had a little accident on the seat of his new car.*

Felix was not entirely sure that having an accident in a car was the sort of thing you could make jokes about, but Mo assured him that it was – and if Mo said it was ok, that was good enough for him.

Ned scanned the pictures into the computer, and Felix printed off copies, which Mo used to make mock-ups of the ten cards they had finally selected. She chose a quirky font for the caption that seemed to work rather well and Felix showed the results to his uncle the next time he called round.

'I'm impressed,' he said, after looking through the cards, chuckling as he did so. 'Old photos . . . I think you could be on to something there!' He looked up. 'You're sure your gran doesn't mind you using them?'

'She thinks it's great,' Felix assured him. 'She didn't even want any money.'

'Well, that's extremely generous of her.' Uncle Rufus studied the photos again. 'The printing's going to be the tricky bit. I'm not sure you can get the quality you'll need from the machine you've got at the moment.'

The same thought had already occurred to Felix. The printer in the dining room had produced excellent copies of Mo's pen and ink drawings, but the photographs he had printed on it were not as sharp as he had hoped and Mo said they also needed a glossier finish.

'You think we'll need to buy a new printer?' he asked.

'I'm not sure,' said his uncle. 'I don't know anything about printing, really.' He looked at Felix. 'But when you don't know how to do something . . .'

'. . . you find someone who does!' chimed in Felix.

'Exactly!' said his uncle.

Three days later, Uncle Rufus picked up all four partners after school and drove them out to the industrial estate on the south of town where they were met by a cheerful man with ginger hair and a ginger moustache called Mr Minchin. He was the founder and manager of WePrintAnything, and Felix began by showing him the original photos, along with the mock-ups of the cards Mo had done.

'They're good, aren't they?' said Mr Minchin, with the cards spread out on the table in front of him. He pointed to one of them. 'I like this one especially. My mum knitted me a swimming costume when I was a boy. Put me off going to the beach for years!' He sat back in his chair. 'Well now . . . there's two ways you could go about printing these. One is that I sell you a machine that will do the job at the quality you need, but . . . that's not what I'd recommend. I think you'd be better off letting us do the printing for you.'

He went on to explain that, if they were prepared to order a large enough number of cards – say a thousand or so of each of the ten designs – he could do them for a very reasonable price. And the more they ordered, the cheaper the price would be.

'I've been on your website,' he finished up, 'which I thought was very good by the way, and if you were to let me print the other cards for you as well, I could do you an even better deal. I'm pretty sure I could offer you a price that, per card, would be cheaper than the way you're doing them now. It'd be less work for you too. And you wouldn't have to worry about breakdowns or buying the card and the ink because we'd do all that for you.'

The bottom line was that, if they printed two thousand each of the ten new cards, and a thousand of each of the twenty cards that Mo had drawn, Mr Minchin could provide them all – 40,000 cards, plus the envelopes – for a little over £4,000.

Felix thanked him for his time and advice, said he would think about it, and promised he would be in touch as soon as they had made a decision.

Over the weekend, Ellie-Mae went over the figures, and reported on Monday that Mr Minchin was right. She had calculated the cost of printing all the cards at the moment – the price of the ink, the cost of the card itself, and William's wages – and reckoned that it would be almost six per cent cheaper to get them printed at WePrintAnything.

At the partnership meeting at the end of July, when Ellie-Mae reported that they had sold 789 packs of cards that month, and made a profit, after expenses, of £5,943, Felix proposed that, instead of sharing out the money among the partners as they usually did, they should spend the majority of it on an order of pre-printed cards from Mr Minchin.

He had the mock-ups of the new cards for the adults to look at, explained the need for a different printing method, talked about how much they would save by ordering in quantity, and sat back to let Uncle Rufus, who was chairing the meeting, put it to the vote.

Before he could do so, however, Mo's mother raised a hand.

'What happens,' she asked, 'if you buy all these cards, and they *don't* sell?'

'In that case,' said Felix, 'we'll have lost our money, but—'

'It is quite a lot of money to lose,' said Ned's father.

'I know, but—'

'It is a great deal of money to lose,' said Ellie-Mae's grandmother, who had, as far as Felix could remember, never spoken at a partnership meeting before. 'It is thousands of pounds!'

In no time, there was a rambling discussion about whether it was wise or even necessary to risk such a large sum. Ned's father wondered if it wasn't possible to do a sort of trial run first, and Mo's mother agreed that it would be much better to get a small amount of cards printed to see if they sold and then, if they did, to order a larger number.

It was the sort of thing, Felix thought, that reminded

him why he had not wanted any of their parents to be involved in the first place.

'If we only have a few cards printed,' he explained, 'they will cost us three, maybe four times as much. And if we do a trial run, and it *is* successful, and suddenly lots of people order the cards, we won't be able to send them any, will we? Because it takes a week or ten days for Mr Minchin to process an order.'

Ned's father, however, was still not convinced and the other adults seemed to be siding with him, until Felix's mother stepped in.

'What do you think, Rufus?' she asked. 'Do you think spending this much money is a risk?'

All eyes turned to Uncle Rufus, who did not usually voice an opinion at these meetings. He always said it was not his job to make suggestions. As chairman, his role was simply to find out what the partners wanted to do and let them vote on it.

'Well, we all know it's a risk,' he said, after a pause, 'but then *all* business is a risk, isn't it? Personally, I think these cards are rather good, but that's not a guarantee that they'll sell. Felix thinks they will, though, and he seems to have been right about a lot of things so far.'

'So you'd vote in favour of spending the money, would you?' It was Felix's mother again.

'I don't have a vote,' said Uncle Rufus. 'I'm not one of the partners, remember? But . . . if I was . . . yes, I'd vote for spending the money.'

And that was the end of the discussion really.

Everyone knew that Uncle Rufus was the expert in all matters where business was concerned, and if he thought the risk was worth taking, then not even Ned's father was going to argue with him. Uncle Rufus, after all, was the man whose whole career seemed to have been one business success after another.

Though, interestingly, Felix was shortly to discover that there was one part of his uncle's life that could not be described as a success at all.

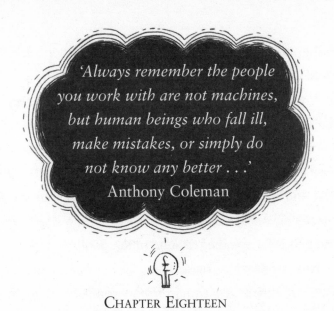

'*Always remember the people you work with are not machines, but human beings who fall ill, make mistakes, or simply do not know any better . . .*'
Anthony Coleman

## CHAPTER EIGHTEEN

# Business Relations

The grounds of Uncle Rufus's house, as well as having a boating lake, a tennis court and several acres of woodland, had a swimming pool. It was housed in a building fifty metres or so from the main house, with glass doors along one side that you could slide open when the weather was warm enough. At the start of the summer holidays, Uncle Rufus had told Felix that he was free to use the pool whenever he wanted – and that if any of the other partners in Kardmart or their families, wanted to use it as well, they would be more than welcome.

'Ludmila uses it for her exercise classes once a week,'

he explained, 'otherwise it's only sitting there. It'd be good to see someone enjoying it.'

It was a generous offer, and the two people who made the most use of it were Felix and Mo. Throughout the summer holiday, Mo's mother drove them out there at least twice a week – though she was always careful to call first and make sure it was convenient – and she would usually sit on one of the loungers reading a book while Mo and Felix splashed around in the pool.

It was on one of these visits, sitting out on the grass after an exhausting game of who could swim furthest under the water, that Mo said, 'She's not happy, is she?'

'Who's not happy?' asked Felix.

Mo pointed to where Ludmila had emerged from the house and was striding towards the lake, her arms folded tightly across her chest.

'There's something wrong between her and your uncle, and she's not happy.'

Felix peered across the grass. 'She looks OK to me.'

'Well, she's not. I reckon they've been arguing again.'

'What do you mean "again"?' Felix frowned. 'I've never heard them arguing. I've never heard them argue about anything.'

'They don't do it in front of us. And especially not in front of you. But you don't have to hear it to know it's happening.'

Mo was still gazing across at Ludmila. 'I lived with that sort of thing for two years before Dad left, remember.'

Felix found it difficult to believe, but three days later, on their next visit to the pool, he discovered Mo was right – as she so often was about such things.

Ludmila had brought out some drinks on a tray for them when they arrived, and Felix was the one who had volunteered to take the glasses back to the kitchen. He could hear the two of them arguing – and not just arguing, but really shouting at each other – as soon as he opened the door. They stopped when they saw him and there was an embarrassed silence for a moment, before Ludmila turned on her heel and walked out of the kitchen.

'I'll take that, shall I?' Uncle Rufus came across to collect the tray, and Felix watched uncertainly as his uncle carried it over to the dishwasher. 'No need to look so worried!' His uncle smiled. 'Just having a bit of a row. Like couples do, I'm afraid. Even your parents, I expect!'

Felix was not sure how to answer that. The truth was that his parents didn't row. They might get cross about something occasionally, or feel a bit down, or get upset when something bad happened, but they never had rows that involved shouting at each other the way his uncle and Ludmila had been.

'Not really,' he said.

'No?' His uncle looked curiously at Felix. 'They must quarrel sometimes! Everybody does!'

Felix tried to remember any occasion on which he had heard his parents quarrel. 'There was one time,' he said eventually, 'about three years ago, when Dad went off to work without giving Mum a goodbye kiss. She was quite upset about that.'

Uncle Rufus was loading the glasses into the dishwasher, but stopped to look at his nephew. 'Are you saying the only time you've heard your parents row was three years ago?'

'It wasn't a row exactly, but Mum was quite upset.'

'And what happened?'

'Well, when Dad came home he said he was sorry and he put a notice up by the door so he'd never forget again.'

'That was it? That was the row?'

'It was quite bad at the time,' said Felix.

'And that was three years ago?'

'Um . . . yes. About that.'

Uncle Rufus closed the dishwasher and stood up, a slightly puzzled expression on his face. 'I wonder how they do it,' he said.

'I could ask them if you like,' said Felix.

'That . . . might not be a good idea in the circumstances.' His uncle rubbed thoughtfully at the back of his neck. 'Although I'd very much like to know what their secret is.' He sighed. 'Or maybe there isn't one. Perhaps you just have to be a different sort of person. I don't know. I just . . . don't know.'

Felix was never quite sure afterwards why he said what he said next. It came out almost without thinking.

'When you don't know how to do something,' he said, 'you find someone who does.'

His uncle looked up sharply, and Felix worried that he might have said something rude.

'I'm sorry. I didn't mean to—'

'No, no, you're quite right,' his uncle interrupted. 'Maybe there *are* people who know about that sort of thing. I never really thought about it . . .'

His voice trailed off, and he stared out into the distance. He was still staring when Mo's mother came in to say it was time for them to leave, and thanked him again for letting them use the pool.

Two days later, Uncle Rufus called round to Felix's house to check that the 40,000 cards from WePrintAnything had been delivered as promised, and that there was enough room in Felix's house to store them.

'If there isn't,' he said, 'you're welcome to keep some at my place.'

'That's very kind,' said Felix, 'but we're OK. Mo's taken about half. She's put them in the spare room at her house.'

'And the quality?' said Uncle Rufus. 'They look OK, do they?'

'I think they look amazing,' Felix assured him, and he was about to say that he would bring some down for his uncle to see, when his mother appeared and asked, as she always did when Uncle Rufus called round, if he would like to stay to supper. And he answered, as he usually did these days, that yes, thank you, he would.

It was, in many ways, a very ordinary evening, with everyone sitting round the table, talking, joking, and sharing the news of their day. Felix passed around copies of the newly printed cards for everyone to admire. William had cooked a spaghetti carbonara and gave them all a little lecture on how the secret of a carbonara was to use proper Pecorino Romano cheese. His mother told them about a woman at the surgery who was spending literally hundreds of pounds on care for her daughter's sick hamster – 'It wasn't even a *nice* hamster,' she said. 'I don't know how they can bear to waste the money' – and his father described the problems he had had felling a windblown oak that morning, nearly killing two dog walkers who had ignored all the warning signs that said to keep out of the woods.

Uncle Rufus was quieter than usual, Felix noticed, and spent a lot of the time gazing round the table at the others with that same puzzled expression on his face that he had had standing by the dishwasher two days before.

When it was time to leave, he thanked William for the meal, congratulated Felix again on his new cards, and said his goodbyes to Felix's mother and father. Out in the hall, he paused by the front door and, reaching out his fingers, touched a piece of faded card pinned to the door frame, which read *Don't forget to give Lois a kiss.*

Felix's father saw the gesture and gave an embarrassed laugh. 'There's a bit of a story about that,' he said.

'Yes, I know,' said Uncle Rufus. 'Felix told me.'

And without turning round he set off down the path to his car.

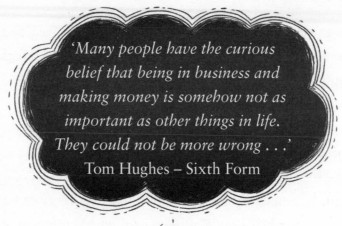

'Many people have the curious belief that being in business and making money is somehow not as important as other things in life. They could not be more wrong . . .'
Tom Hughes – Sixth Form

CHAPTER NINETEEN

# Business Studies

When the new cards were launched at the end of August, there was an immediate surge in sales.

Ned and Mo had done a great job sorting out the new pages that were required for the website. As well as putting up pictures of the new cards, they had revamped the site's overall layout. Using some of the 5FW characters from Mo's original cards, she and Ned had brought two of them to life as animations. Now, when you clicked on the home page, one character would shuffle on from one side, holding up his trousers with one hand and waving with the other, and a girl would come on from the other side and give you a silly grin. All of the pages had some-thing similar and the result made Felix smile every time he looked at them.

They had more than 350 orders in the first week – 162 of them for the new cards – and by the end of the month that total had reached 1,204. A monthly turnover of more than £12,000 was, as Uncle Rufus said, enough to keep most small businesses happy, and certainly justified the £4,000 they had spent on having the cards printed professionally.

It was inevitable that news of Kardmart's success should leak out eventually to the wider world. Although the four partners were sensible enough never to talk much about it themselves, it was not the sort of thing you could keep secret indefinitely. Whether it was from something Mo or Ned said, or something passed around the family and then to friends, word slowly spread about the four thirteen-year-old children who had, apparently, set up a business on the internet and made a small fortune.

Then, one day in late September, there was a phone call from the local newspaper, followed by an article in the *Advertiser* with the headline 'Child Stars of Business Enterprise'. And after that, everybody knew.

The reaction at school was not quite what Felix

had expected. Among his fellow students, most were surprised, some were a little envious – though Felix always did his best, when people asked him about it, to give the impression he didn't make *that* much money – and some were simply curious about how he had done it.

But the odd thing – though it was a while before Felix noticed it – was that his teachers never spoke about it at all. It was odd, because the school was usually very careful to acknowledge the achievements of its students. When a boy in Felix's year had made it into the Southern Area judo team, he had been called up on stage in assembly and applauded. Anyone who had done well in sport, or art, or music, got the same treatment and their achievements were duly celebrated. But for some reason setting up a business that sold thousands of greetings cards didn't seem to count.

The only time that one of his teachers spoke to Felix about it was when the deputy head, a lean, hawk-faced woman, called him into her office. Mrs Rawlings had a copy of the local paper on her desk and said she wanted to remind him that conducting any commercial enterprise on school premises was strictly against the rules. She also wrote a letter to his parents saying that anything that impacted adversely on his school work would be taken extremely seriously, and reminding them that regular attendance at school was a legal requirement. The parents of Mo, Ned and Ellie-Mae got the same letter.

There was a distinct air of disapproval in Mrs Rawlings' voice as she spoke. As if she didn't really think Felix should be doing something like setting up a business instead of concentrating on his school work. It puzzled him. The school didn't mind if you had a job delivering newspapers or if you worked in a shop on a Saturday. Nobody disapproved if you spent three hours a day practising the piano, or doing football practice, or reading books about science – they seemed to think any of those things were fine. So why was running a business different? Why wasn't it treated the same way?

It meant that when one teacher *didn't* treat it as something different, it came as a welcome surprise. Felix was coming out of the dining room one lunch break in the autumn term when a short, stocky man with a cheerful smile came up to him.

'Felix Farmer?' he said. 'My name's Tom Hughes and I teach economics and business studies over in the sixth form. Could we talk?'

It was a sunny day and they sat on a bench outside the staff room and Mr Hughes produced a set of Kardmart's cards from his pocket.

'I ordered some of your cards a week ago,' he said.

'There's nothing wrong with them, is there?' asked Felix.

'Nothing at all. They arrived exactly when they were promised, my wife says they're a bargain, and I think they're brilliant.' Mr Hughes smiled across at Felix. 'Is it true that you set up the business on your own?'

Felix admitted that the idea had indeed been his and, for the next half hour, Mr Hughes quizzed him about how exactly it had happened, how the first cards had been sold and how the partnership had been formed. He was particularly interested in the bit about how most of it had been done without his parents even knowing, and how setting up the website had been the real launch pad.

'It's a remarkable story,' he said, when Felix had finished. 'I wonder if you'd be prepared to share it with my business studies class. You see, I spend my day talking about how businesses are started, but I think hearing from someone who's actually done it would be much more interesting for them.'

The idea of standing up in front of a class of sixth formers and giving some sort of speech did not really appeal to Felix, and he said so.

'No, no, you wouldn't have to make a speech,' Mr Hughes assured him. 'In fact, you wouldn't even have to stand up. All I want you to do is sit there and answer questions from me, in exactly the way you've just been doing. I promise you'll have a very interested audience. Would you be up for that?'

And Felix said, all right, yes, he would.

The talk was arranged for a month later and it was attended not just by a single class, but by almost the entire sixth form. They filled all the seats in the drama hall and late arrivals were actually sitting on the stairs and in the aisle.

'I hope you don't mind,' said Mr Hughes, 'but there was so much interest that I threw it open to everyone. A lot of people seemed to want to hear your story.'

He began by asking Felix questions, just as he had before, about Kardmart, and the audience listened intently. They laughed when he described how he had got no response at all to the flyers he had sent out, and at the reaction of his parents when they first saw the shoebox full of money on the kitchen table, and were visibly impressed when Mr Hughes got him to reveal how much the partnership was making at the moment.

After thirty minutes, the teacher threw the meeting open to questions, and there were plenty of them. They were mostly about why Felix thought he had succeeded, what he did with the money, his plans for the future and so on, but one question in particular stood out afterwards in Felix's memory. It was at the end of the session and came from an earnest-looking student in the front row.

'Is it enough?' he asked. 'Just making money?'

Felix wasn't sure at first what he meant.

'I don't want to be rude.' The boy glanced nervously at Mr Hughes. 'But the only point of going into business is to make money, right? And if that's all you did with your life – make money – would that be enough? Would that be . . . a worthwhile life?'

It was not something Felix had ever considered, and he had to think about it before he answered.

'I'm not sure,' he said eventually. 'All I know is that I always wanted to set up a successful business. I've wanted it the way some people want to be in a band, or play football, or to be famous on television . . . and when it actually *worked*, when it happened, it was like' – he searched for the words to express what he felt – 'it wasn't just the money. I'm not sure why, but it's the most *satisfying* thing I've ever done.'

'And I'm afraid we're going to have to wrap it up there,' said Mr Hughes. 'But before we do, I would like to pick up on something from that last question. In our business studies classes we often talk about the curious belief that many people have that being in business and making money is somehow not as important as other things in life. That it's less worthy of respect than other professions, when the truth is that our whole civilization rests in large part on businessmen and women and the wealth they create.'

He looked out over the throng of students.

'It's worth remembering that the reason we are able to come to this school and receive an education is that it has been paid for by the wealth created by businessmen and women. The clothes on your back and the food you eat is all provided, in some form, by businessmen and women. The books you read, the television you watch, the cinema you go to – all organized by businessmen and women. When you leave school and look for employment, most of you will find it working for businessmen or women. If you can't find work, or are too old, or are sick, then you will be given a pension or state benefits – and the money for those benefits all comes from taxes paid by those running businesses, like our guest here today.'

He turned to Felix. 'On behalf of the sixth form, I would like to thank you for giving up your time to come and tell us a bit about how you got started and something of your plans for the future. It has been a most stimulating and thoughtful afternoon.'

145

The round of applause that followed was gratifyingly enthusiastic, but Felix was rather distracted by one of the things Mr Hughes had just said and, as soon as he had left the hall, the first thing he did was phone his uncle.

'Uncle Rufus,' he said. 'I don't have to pay taxes, do I?'

'Ah . . .' said his uncle. 'I've been meaning to talk to you about that.'

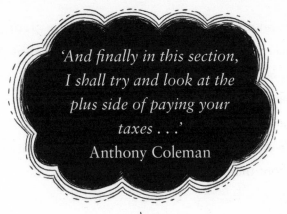

*'And finally in this section, I shall try and look at the plus side of paying your taxes . . .'*

Anthony Coleman

CHAPTER TWENTY

# The Taxman

'Everybody who earns money,' said Uncle Rufus, 'however they earn it, has to give some of it to the government so that they can build hospitals and schools, pay police officers, have an army, all that sort of thing.'

He was sitting at the head of the dining table, with the four partners of Kardmart sitting round the other three sides looking a trifle anxious, as were the only other two adults in the room – Felix's father and Ellie-Mae's grand-mother. Ned's father was away on business, Felix's mother had been called out to an emergency at the surgery, and Mo's mother was in bed with an upset stomach.

'Everybody has to pay?' asked Mo.

'Nearly everybody,' Uncle Rufus corrected himself. 'At the moment you're allowed to earn about four and a half thousand pounds a year without paying any tax, but after that you have to pay a proportion of what you earn to the government. It's called income tax and the more you earn, the more you have to pay. I'm mentioning it now because it's clear that the way the business is doing, all of you will have to pay something after next April.'

'Why April?' asked Ned.

'Because that's the end of the financial year. April the sixth to be exact. That's when you work out how much money you earned in the previous twelve months, and then the government tells you how much tax you have to pay.'

'And how much will it be?' asked Felix.

'At the moment it starts at twenty-five per cent. You have to pay a quarter of what you earn to the Inland Revenue, but it goes up. The more you earn, the more you have to pay, and the people who earn most have to pay forty per cent.'

Felix was shocked. He didn't mind contributing something to help pay for hospitals and so on, but the idea of having to give up almost *half* of the money he made seemed . . . a little unfair.

'And it doesn't stop there, I'm afraid,' his uncle continued. 'If your business is successful and earns more than a certain amount each year, you have to pay VAT as well. That's another seventeen and a half per cent. You won't have to pay it this year, but if the business keeps growing . . . who knows!'

Ned raised a hand. 'Supposing,' he said, 'we didn't tell the government how much we're earning. I mean, if they didn't know—'

'Don't even think about it,' Uncle Rufus interrupted firmly. 'Nobody with any sense messes with the Inland Revenue. If you don't pay your taxes and they find out – and they're very good at finding out – you wind up paying huge fines and going to prison.' He looked at Felix. 'Like your business studies teacher said, taxes pay for a lot of things we all need, and only people who earn a lot have to pay a lot. So cough up and be glad you can afford it.'

'Who has to pay the tax?' asked Ellie-Mae. 'Is it the partnership, or each of us on our own?'

'Good question.' Uncle Rufus smiled at her. 'At the end of the tax year, you will have to submit a report on how much money the partnership has earned – which is why it was so important that you kept all the receipts and figures so carefully – but the tax you all have to pay is worked out individually and depends on how much each of you earned.'

'Do we still have to pay even though we're not adults?' said Mo. 'I mean, aren't we too young?'

'I'm afraid age has nothing to do with it,' said Uncle Rufus. 'Everybody who earns money – however old or young they are – pays tax. Everybody. And you'll need to be ready for it. As a rough rule of thumb, it's a good idea to keep thirty per cent of everything you earn in a separate account, so that you have enough to pay the tax when you have to.'

The faces around him were looking a little glum at this news and Uncle Rufus assured them that there was no need to be disheartened. 'I don't think any of you need to worry too much,' he assured them. 'Not after the monthly report Ellie-Mae gave us!'

The first item on the agenda, as it always was, had been Ellie-Mae's report of how much money the partner-ship had earned in the last month and the news had indeed been most encouraging. Another new set of cards using photographs from Felix's grandmother's collection had gone on sale in November, and the number of orders – which had fallen slightly in the previous month – had gone up again soon after to provide an income that month of £11,560.

'And the good news doesn't stop there, does it, Mo?' Uncle Rufus turned to face her. 'Item three on our agenda is the news that you've finished a new set of drawings – is that right?'

Mo blushed slightly and reached down to a folder by the side of her chair, which she brought out and opened up on the table. 'I'm not sure you'll like them,' she said, 'but, yes, I've done another set of cards.'

Mo had indeed done a new set of drawings of the characters from 5FW. They were mostly based, Felix saw, on things that that he could remember had actually happened at Monmouth Junior. Like the reading period in the library when Barry's ferret had escaped and bitten Dylan (of course). Its jaws had been so firmly locked onto his hand that a vet had to be called in to give it an injection of muscle relaxant and set him free.

Felix's favourite was the drawing of 5FW out on the playing field, doing a re-enactment of an attack by Vikings on a Saxon village.

The caption said: *During 5FW's role play of a Viking raid, Miss Tindall thought there was more pillaging than was really appropriate for a primary school.*

These were almost the exact words the head teacher had used, Felix remembered, and he could still see the look of disapproval on her face as a particularly enthusiastic set of Vikings had carried the beautiful Samar back to their longboat.

'Wonderful stuff,' said Uncle Rufus when he saw them. 'Another set of winners, Mo! Well done!'

And everyone agreed.

There followed a discussion of how many of the new cards they should order from Mr Minchin, and when they should come out. The decision was taken to launch them as soon as possible after Christmas, and then they talked about which of the other cards they should have reprinted at the same time. At the end, when Felix proposed that they spend a further £5,000 with WePrintAnything, the vote in favour was unanimous.

It was, despite the news of the tax they would have to pay, a remarkably cheery meeting.

When it was over, Felix's mother asked Uncle Rufus if he would like to stay for supper, but he said that this time he could not.

'I'm taking Ludmila out to dinner tonight,' he explained, moving out to the hall to collect his coat. 'To the Hotel du Vin.'

'Are you now?' Mrs Farmer was impressed. The Hotel du Vin was an extremely expensive restaurant. 'Special occasion, is it?'

'As a matter of fact, it is.' Uncle Rufus looked faintly embarrassed. 'Yesterday I asked Ludmila to marry me and she said yes. So tonight we're going out to celebrate.'

'Oh, that is wonderful news!' Felix's mother beamed enthusiastically. 'Congratulations! She's so lovely – and I'm sure you'll be very happy together.'

'If we're not,' said Uncle Rufus, pulling open the front door, 'you can blame Felix. He's the one responsible.'

And with a wave, he set off down to the path to his car.

'Blame Felix?' Mrs Farmer stared after him for a moment before turning back to her son. 'Why would he think you were the one responsible?'

But Felix had no idea why his uncle had said that, or what he had meant.

No idea at all.

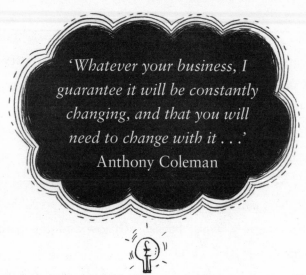

'Whatever your business, I guarantee it will be constantly changing, and that you will need to change with it . . .'
Anthony Coleman

## CHAPTER TWENTY ONE

# Debits and Credits

The new cards went on sale soon after the New Year, and Felix prepared carefully for the launch. Ned had the new pages for the website set up and ready to run, Mo had done a sort of banner over the home page saying that new cards by the award-winning Mo Burnley would shortly be on sale, and Felix wrote the email that was sent out to everyone on the mailing list telling them when the cards would be available.

The result was a gratifying and dramatic lift in sales. They had 142 orders on the first day – which certainly kept William busy – and a further 319 orders by the end of the week. Felix took the news round to Mo on Sunday afternoon and found her up in the spare bedroom, which had recently been converted into her full-time art studio.

There were new shelves and drawers all along one wall, holding reams of paper, and sets of paints and pens and inks. There was a new drawing desk and chair at one end of the room under the window, and a sofa along the wall opposite that had replaced the bed.

Mo was at the desk working on a drawing which she covered up as soon as Felix came into the room.

'Four hundred and sixty-one orders?' she said, when Felix told her. 'How much money would that be? For me, I mean.'

'Well, it's just over four and a half thousand pounds,' said Felix, 'and you get thirty-five per cent of that, so . . . you'll get about fifteen hundred pounds. Roughly.'

'Wow . . .' Mo smiled. 'Fifteen hundred pounds in one week!'

'It's good, isn't it!' Felix sat himself on the sofa and looked round the room, at the new furniture and at the shelves brimming with art supplies. There wasn't much doubt about where Mo spent most of the money she earned, he thought, though there had been a brief period in the autumn when her mother had tried to insist that she not buy anything without asking her permission first. It had caused some fierce arguments and it was Uncle Rufus who had – at Mo's mother's request – negotiated a compromise. They had worked out a deal where, in future, any money Mo earned would be divided into three equal parts. One third would be put aside for tax, one third would go into savings, and the final third would be for Mo to spend in any way she wished. It seemed to give her enough to buy most of the things she wanted, Felix thought.

'And how much do you get?' Mo asked, coming over to sit beside Felix on the sofa.

'This week? My share's a bit over two thousand.'

'Which you probably won't spend on anything, will you? You'll just put it into savings, with all the rest of your money.'

'Probably,' Felix agreed. 'But that's because there's nothing I particularly want to spend it on at the moment. Uncle Rufus says he's going to find somewhere for me to invest it until there is.'

'You are going to be *so* rich!' Mo leaned her head back against the sofa. 'I can see it now . . . you are going to be this mega-rich tycoon at the head of a business empire . . . Felix Farmer Limited!'

'Well . . .'

'No, scrub that! It's going to be Felix *Un*limited!'

Mo turned her head to face him. 'Are you going to get married? I don't mean now, obviously, I mean . . . sometime.'

'Um . . . I don't know.' Felix did not always find it easy to keep up with his friend's thought processes. 'Probably. One day. Why?'

'Well, I was thinking when you *are* incredibly rich, and you decide you need a wife . . . let me know, and I'll dump whoever I'm with and you can marry me. OK?'

'What a very generous offer,' said Felix. 'Thank you.'

At the partnership meeting at the end of January, Ellie-Mae revealed that the total sales for that month were a record £15,440. It was cheering news, but perhaps more significant for the business was the decision they took to switch from payment in cash on the Kardmart website, to payment by credit or debit card.

Uncle Rufus had been quietly urging this move for some time. He had pointed out more than once that, although it would involve some expense, this would be more than covered simply by the saving on postage. It would also cut down on the number of people who didn't pay, and the need to keep checking on who *had* paid and who had not and needed to be sent a reminder.

Felix was, privately, a little sad to see the end of the

brown envelopes with the ten-pound notes inside that dropped on the doorstep each morning. He had liked the way the money piled up in the box under his bed – the way you could look at it and touch it before it was taken down to the bank. But, as his uncle said, payment by card was an obvious improvement to the smooth running of the business and the change was unanimously agreed on.

It was a change that brought one important and unexpected consequence. Felix's brother, William, had established a very happy pattern of life. The work he did for Kardmart gave him money in his pocket, plenty of time to do the cooking he had always enjoyed, and in his spare time he had recently joined a ukulele orchestra that met three evenings a week and did concerts around the county at weekends. Now, however, this comfortable way of life was under threat.

The amount of work that William needed to do had already been reduced by the introduction of pre-printed cards and, once the customers of Kardmart paid by credit or debit card, it was reduced even further. There was no longer any need to open brown envelopes and count the money and record who had sent it. These days, when someone placed an order, all William had to do was take the cards out of a box, put them in a padded envelope, stick on the pre-printed address label and a stamp, and take it down to the post. The whole thing could often be done in less than an hour and, as William was paid on the number of hours he worked, the amount he was paid each week had fallen dramatically.

'I've been wondering,' Felix told his uncle, 'if there was anything else we could give him to do.'

'Like what?'

'I don't know,' said Felix. 'But we could find him something, couldn't we? He needs the money.'

'If your brother needs more money,' said Uncle Rufus briskly, 'that's for him to sort out, not you. He's a grown man, and if he wants to earn more, he can go out and find another job.'

Two days later, Felix found that his brother had already done exactly that. A girl he knew from the ukulele orchestra worked at a small bakery, where the man who owned the business and did most of the baking had recently had a heart attack. What he needed was someone young and energetic to do the heavy work for him, and the girl wondered if it was the sort of thing William might be interested in.

'So I went down and had a word with her boss,' he told Felix, 'and he's offered me the job. I can still do all the work here for you though. I finish at the bakery at two o'clock, so I can come back and do all the card stuff for you then, if you want.'

'That's great,' said Felix. 'When do you start?'

'On Monday. But I have to have two references. And one of them has to be from my previous employer.'

'You mean the tea factory?' said Felix.

'No,' said William. 'I mean you. You're my previous employer. And if you could do it for me today, please, because I said I'd take it in tomorrow.'

Felix wasn't entirely sure what a reference was, and had no idea how to write one, so he phoned his uncle.

'Was your brother fairly hard-working when he was doing the cards for you?' asked Uncle Rufus.

'Yes, very hard-working.'

'And was he reliable? Did he turn up when he said he would, and do what he said he was going to do?'

'Always.'

'And you could trust him not to run off with the money? He didn't steal anything?'

'No, of course not!'

'Then that's what you write,' said Uncle Rufus.

So Felix wrote a paragraph that said his brother was reliable, hard-working, and trustworthy – and William started at the bakery the next Monday. His day began at five in the morning, and the work was hot, heavy and demanding. It was not the sort of job that everyone would have been prepared to do – but William loved it.

He would come home soon after two o'clock each day, usually clutching a couple of loaves and a box of buns or a cake of some sort, and at the evening meal – which he still cooked – talk eagerly of all he had learned during the day.

He had, Felix thought, never seen his brother so happy.

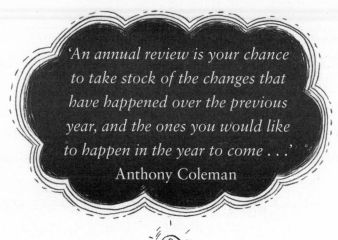

*'An annual review is your chance to take stock of the changes that have happened over the previous year, and the ones you would like to happen in the year to come . . .'*
Anthony Coleman

CHAPTER TWENTY TWO

# Annual Review

In the partnership meeting at the end of February, Ellie-Mae reported that, in the last four weeks, they had sold 10,140 cards. It was fewer than the month before, but that was something Felix had half expected once the first rush for Mo's new cards was over. In March there was another slight fall in the numbers – income was a little over £9,000 – but the trend turned back up again in April, boosted by the release of another set of the cards with photos.

At the meeting at the end of April, as well as the monthly figures, Ellie-Mae produced the partnership's first Annual Financial Report. It would be needed, as Uncle Rufus had explained, for tax reasons, and showed that in the twelve months up to April the sixth Kardmart had sold 72,410 cards, and made a profit after expenses of £53,894.47. While everyone was absorbing this news, Uncle Rufus gave a little speech, congratulating them all on such a splendid achievement.

'I can remember,' he said, 'Felix coming out to my house almost exactly a year ago and telling me the story of how Kardmart got started. How he got the idea of selling Mo's wonderful cards, then got Ned to build a website, and Ellie-Mae to look after the accounts. And I remember how impressed I was by hearing what you had all done . . . and I look round the room now and see what you've done since, and how you've all grown and how confident you've become – and I'm more impressed than ever! It has been the most wonderful adventure, and I feel privileged to have been a part of it. I congratulated you all a year ago, and I'll do the same again today. Well done! *Very* well done!'

And he finished up by saying how much he looked forward to seeing them all the following Saturday which, in case any of them had forgotten, was the day he and Ludmila were getting married.

\*

All four Kardmart partners had been invited to the wedding – along with their parents or, in Ellie-Mae's case, her grandmother – and it was, by any standards, a memorable occasion.

The ceremony itself took place at St Peters, in town – Ludmila was a Catholic – and after that everyone moved back to Uncle Rufus's house, where three marquees had been set up on the lawns in front of the lake. One of them was large enough for the several hundred guests to sit down and eat, the second had a band playing music for anyone who felt like dancing, and the third contained a dozen dodgem cars hired from a fairground.

The swimming pool was open for anyone who fancied a swim, and the lake had been provided with a collection of rowing boats, canoes and pedalos, along with some smiling young men standing discreetly nearby with life-guard signs on their chests. From start to finish, a small army of waiters and waitresses were constantly on the move ensuring nobody was without a drink, while a small team of photographers recorded it all.

Felix's father was best man – *Just make sure he turns up this time*, his wife had been heard to mutter – and gave a speech with several stories of what Rufus had been like when he was younger, but mostly saying how proud he was of his brother's achievements and how pleased he had been to hear that he was going to marry someone as beautiful, clever and kind as Ludmila.

It was a happy occasion, but the most memorable part of it for Felix came in the evening, after the meal and the speeches were over. He was standing in front of the swimming pool – he'd arranged to meet Mo there – and he was looking out over the lake and at the hundreds of guests moving around between the tents, when Ludmila came across, still wearing what had to be the shortest wedding dress ever.

'I am glad I found you, Felix,' she said. 'I have a present for you.'

And she produced a parcel, carefully wrapped in silver paper. Felix opened it to find one of Mo's drawings, beautifully framed. It was a picture of himself sitting in a chair behind a huge desk in the penthouse office of a sky-scraper, shouting into a phone, while his minions (clearly recognizable as Ned, Ellie-Mae and Mo), scurried around the office doing his bidding.

'I hope you like it,' said Ludmila. 'I wanted to give you something to say thank you.'

'It's fantastic,' said Felix, 'but . . . thank me for what?'

'All this . . .' Ludmila waved an arm in a gesture that took in the lawns, the lake and the people. 'We all know it would never have happened without you.'

'Do we?'

'Because you are the one who told him,' said Ludmila, 'and I think you were the only one who *could* have told him. He would not have listened to anyone else. And I am so grateful.' His new aunt leant forward as she spoke, and gave him a kiss on the cheek.

'You've got lipstick all over you,' said Mo disapprovingly, when she arrived a few minutes later. 'Hold still.' She took out a hankie, licked it, and then used it to wipe his cheek.

'Ludmila seems to think I'm the one who told Uncle Rufus to get married,' he said.

'Yes, I know,' said Mo. 'And you were.'

'No, I wasn't! I didn't tell him anything!'

'Yes, you did. In a way.' The two of them sat down together on the grass. 'You remember that day in the summer when we were out here for a swim and you found them arguing? You told your uncle that he should get some proper advice.'

Felix had no difficulty remembering the occasion, but . . . had he really told his uncle to 'get some proper advice'? Perhaps, without meaning to, he had . . .

'That's why he went to counselling,' Mo continued, 'and that's when he and Ludmila started really talking about what they both wanted, and he found out what Ludmila really wanted was to get married and have children.'

'Is that what she was upset about?'

'It was a big part of it, yes.'

Felix stared at her. 'How do you *know* all these things?' he asked.

Mo gave a shrug, but did not answer. Instead, she pointed to the picture in his hands. 'Do you like it?'

'It's brilliant,' said Felix. 'Did she pay you for it?'

'Well, I would have done it for nothing,' said Mo, 'but then I thought . . .'

'How much?'

'Two hundred and fifty pounds,' said Mo. 'She wanted to pay five hundred, but that's what we settled on.'

Felix stared admiringly at his friend, and thought how much she had changed in the last year. He could remember how quiet and withdrawn she had been after her father had left, and then how hard it had been for her to cope with her mother's depression. And now . . . Well, when your cards are being sold all over the country, and you can charge £250 for a drawing, you probably couldn't help but feel a bit more confident.

And it wasn't just Mo, he thought, catching a glimpse of Ned, down by the lake, talking earnestly to a middle-aged man in a suit. Ned now ran a business of his own, build-ing websites for people. It had started when Mr Minchin had asked if he could do one for WePrintAnything. It was a time when all sorts of businesses were suddenly realizing that they needed to be on this new internet thing, and there was a distinct shortage of people who could make that happen. Word had quickly got round locally that Ned, despite his age, had the skills required, and with Mo's advice on the artistic/design front, he was making a small fortune. Felix smiled as he watched Ned produce a business card and pass it over to the man in the suit, who thanked him and tucked it carefully into his pocket.

They had all changed, he thought, even Ellie-Mae, who he could see sitting outside one of the tents talking to members of the band. Two evenings before he had seen her walk out onto the stage at school and give a solo cello recital with a self-assurance that had impressed everyone. Not that he was surprised. Ellie-Mae gave her monthly reports to the partnership these days with a similar confidence and Felix couldn't help thinking that being part of a successful business had something to do with it.

And Kardmart had affected more than the partners. He could see his brother William, climbing into a canoe with his ukulele-playing friend from the bakery. His new job was going well, and these days they did more than offer a choice of white bread or brown. William had been experimenting with new loaves – sourdough, rye, brioche and ciabattas – and found there was a highly profitable market for them. Kardmart might not have caused any of that directly, but it had certainly helped.

And over by the house, he could see Uncle Rufus with his mother and father, all posing for someone to take yet another photo. They had their arms round each other's shoulders and were laughing, and he remembered his mother saying that of all the good things to come out of his card business, the best of them had been the way it had brought the two brothers back together.

The business had indeed affected them all, Felix thought, and he wondered if it had changed him too. He didn't feel any different, but maybe it had. He had certainly learned a lot. And the changes, as his uncle had pointed out at the last partnership meeting, had all started from that single moment when he had wondered if selling Mo's cards might be a good idea for a business. Everything that had happened since had spread out, like ripples in a pond, from that single decision.

'Your uncle was right,' said Mo, threading her arm through his. 'At the meeting last week. When he said it had all been a wonderful adventure.'

'Yes,' Felix agreed. 'Yes, it has.'

Which made it all the more of a shock, of course, when the whole thing suddenly came to an end.

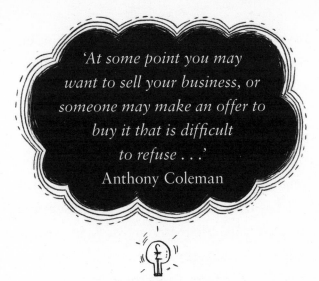

'At some point you may want to sell your business, or someone may make an offer to buy it that is difficult to refuse . . .'
Anthony Coleman

## CHAPTER TWENTY THREE

# The Offer

Sales dipped slightly in May – they sold 8,320 cards – and in June they were down again to 7,140. Although there was still a lot of money coming in, Felix remembered his uncle saying once that if your business was not expanding and growing, then it was dying – and he did not want Kardmart to die.

'I don't think you need to be too concerned yet,' said Uncle Rufus when he saw the figures. 'All businesses have their ups and downs. Sometimes you just have to wait for the wheel to turn back in your favour.'

He did suggest, though, that Felix might like to ask his

customers if there was anything they wanted his business to provide that it was not already doing.

So in July, at the start of the summer holidays, Felix sent out an email questionnaire to all the people who had ordered cards from him, and while most of the replies he got said they were more than happy with the service Kardmart provided, some people said they did not always want to buy ten cards. They would prefer, sometimes, to buy whatever number they wanted. Some went further and said they would also like to be able to choose which cards they bought from across the entire range.

These would not, Felix knew, be simple changes to make. One of the main reasons Kardmart was able to sell cards so cheaply was that they sold them ten at a time. If Felix let people buy just one or two cards, the cost of extra postage and extra padded envelopes would eat into his profits. And if they were allowed to say which cards they wanted, the time taken to go through all the boxes and find and pack the cards selected would go up as well. It was something he needed to talk over with his uncle.

But his uncle was not available in July, or during most of August. He had taken Ludmila for an extended holiday in her home town of Poprad in Slovakia, and, on his return, had been very caught up in finding new sources for his business providing batteries for forklift trucks.

In the meantime, the sales figures continued to slip down. In July, despite the launch of a new set of the photo cards, sales fell to under 7,000 for the first time in over a year. When Felix showed the figures to his uncle on his return from Poprad, he frowned.

'Well, I agree that *something* must be happening,' he said. 'But I'm not sure what. Leave it with me, will you? There's a couple of people I've been planning to talk to, and maybe one of them will come up with an answer. I'll be in touch, OK?'

Felix did not hear from his uncle for three weeks after that, and then, a week before the end of the summer holidays, Uncle Rufus phoned to say that he had some news at last.

'I think I know what's happening,' he said, 'and I've got a suggestion for what you might do about it, but I'm off to Poland this afternoon. Back on Wednesday. How about I called in then? You're not at school or anything yet, are you?'

'Term starts on Thursday,' Felix told him. 'Wednesday would be fine.'

'Good. I'll be with you by two p.m. I'll explain my idea then, and you'll have a few days to think about it before the partnership meeting on Saturday. See you Wednesday!'

Felix put down the phone, wondering what it was that his uncle had discovered and what his 'idea' might be.

At two o'clock on Wednesday, however, there was no sign of Uncle Rufus. Felix waited for an hour, and then rang his house to find out what had happened.

Ludmila answered the phone. 'You haven't seen the news?' she said. 'He's still in Bzerg.'

'What news?' asked Felix.

'It's the floods. Half of Poland's under water and Bzerg is cut off. They've got no electricity. Nothing!'

'Oh,' said Felix. 'Is Uncle Rufus all right?'

Ludmila laughed. 'He is probably making money selling everyone life jackets!' she said. 'He is fine. But he can't get out. What did you want him for?'

Felix explained that they had arranged to meet that afternoon.

'Of course, yes! He was going to tell you about the offer, wasn't he? So you had time to think about it before Saturday . . . Hold on!'

Felix could hear the sound of his aunt's heels clicking down a corridor.

'I saw something on his desk the other day and . . . Yes, here it is! He had it all typed up ready for you. And there's a letter. I'll get Peter to drive over with it, shall I?'

Peter was the gardener and odd job man who worked for Uncle Rufus, and an hour later he appeared outside Felix's house with a brown manila envelope, which he passed to a waiting Felix.

It contained four copies of a twelve-page document covered in closely typed writing, and four copies of a letter from his uncle addressed to all the partners, which said:

*Dear Felix, Mo, Ned and Ellie-Mae,*

*I hope the attached document will please you! Felix will have explained what it is about and why we think it is a good offer, but you may want to look through the fine print (and get your parents or guardians to do the same) before we discuss it on Saturday at the partnership meeting.*

*For various reasons, I don't think we have a lot of time on this one. The offer is a generous one and I'm not sure how long it will be on the table. If we are going to accept it (and Felix will have told you that I think we should) then the sooner the better!*

*With very best wishes,*

*Rufus Farmer*

Felix read the letter twice and was puzzled. It was the first he had heard of an 'offer' – presumably it was what his uncle had been planning to tell him about – and he had to read through all twelve pages of the proposed contract twice before he had much idea what the offer was.

It came from a company called Gainsborough – Felix knew they were one of the biggest producers of greetings cards in the UK – who wanted to buy Kardmart.

And they were offering a quarter of a million pounds.

Felix passed on the copies of the contract and Rufus's letter to the others at school the next day. They met at lunchtime in one of the music practice rooms, which had the advantage of being both quiet and private.

Mo looked at the twelve pages of fine print and did not even attempt to read it. 'What does it say?' she asked.

Felix told her it was an offer to buy Kardmart for £250,000.

'Wow . . .' Mo's eyes widened. 'How much would—'

'Your share would be £81,250,' said Ellie-Mae. She turned to Ned. 'We would get £31,250 each.'

Ned gave a low whistle. 'Well . . . that's my university fees sorted!'

'Felix?' said Mo. 'You don't look very excited about it.'

'No,' said Felix, 'I'm not.'

He had worked out the night before that his share of the £250,000 would be exactly £106,250. It was a lot of money, but the more he thought about it, the more he knew that selling the business was not what he wanted to do, and he did not understand why his uncle should think that it was.

For Felix, running Kardmart – watching the business grow, dealing with the problems, working out what to do next – wasn't something he did simply to make money. It was something he enjoyed – enjoyed enormously. Doing it was a central part of his life. Why would anyone think he wanted to give it up?

The money might seem to be a good reason, but Felix had spent the previous evening going over the figures and, although a quarter of a million might sound like an attractive offer, turning it down did not mean they would necessarily be worse off. As he pointed out to the others, Kardmart was still bringing in over £6,000 each month and, even if sales fell a bit, he calculated that in four or five years' time they would have made the same money they were being offered now, and still have the business.

And that was only if profits went down a bit more. Supposing they didn't? Supposing they went up? The more he thought about it, the more sure Felix was that he did not want to sell Kardmart to anyone.

'Your uncle says he thinks we should take the offer,' said Ellie-Mae.

'I know,' said Felix.

'Why does he think it's such a good deal?' asked Mo.

'I don't know,' Felix told her. 'I suppose he's going to explain it to us at the partnership meeting on Saturday.'

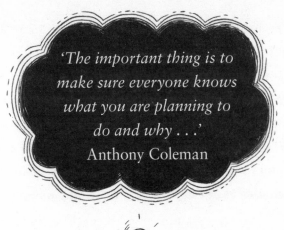

'The important thing is to make sure everyone knows what you are planning to do and why . . .'
Anthony Coleman

CHAPTER TWENTY FOUR

# Sold Out

On Saturday, however, Ludmila phoned to say that Uncle Rufus was still out of the country.

'As far as I can tell,' she told him, 'he made it as far as Warsaw, but still hasn't managed to get a flight to the UK. He was planning to try and get back via Paris, but it's chaos out there. I'm not sure where he is at the moment.'

Felix suggested postponing the meeting, but Ned's father was flying to Japan for three weeks the next day, and asked if they could stick with the original timetable, even without Uncle Rufus. So, with Felix in the chair, they gathered round the dining-room table as usual, and the partnership meeting went ahead.

They began with the report of sales that month, which were very slightly down again, but August was, as Felix pointed out, not a good month for selling anything except ice cream. Item two was a brief discussion of the response to the survey Felix had sent out – they decided to wait until Uncle Rufus was back before making any big decisions about it – and item three on the agenda was the offer from Gainsborough.

Felix said he thought, again, that there was not much point discussing this without his uncle, and suggested that voting on this item be postponed as well.

'Personally,' he added, 'I don't want to sell at all, but we'll wait and hear what my uncle has to say, shall we?'

He was about to move on to the next item on the agenda – how many cards they should order from WePrintAnything – when Mo's mother interrupted.

'Your uncle seemed to think it was a good offer,' she said, 'and his letter says we'd need to move quickly.'

'Yes, I know,' said Felix, 'but—'

'And your uncle's a smart man,' put in Ned's father. 'If he recommends we take the offer, he'll have had his reasons.'

'Yes,' Felix agreed, 'but he's not here to tell us what they are, is he? So I think—'

'It says in his letter,' Mo's mother interrupted again, 'that he's not sure how long this offer will be on the table. And that the sooner we accept it the better.'

'I know, but—'

'We have enormous respect for you, Felix.' It was Ned's father again. 'I hope you know that. All of us have the greatest admiration for what you've done.' He gestured round the room, and Mo's mother and Ellie-Mae's grandmother nodded their agreement. 'But the thing is, this offer is for a very large sum of money and we think you should take it.'

'Absolutely,' said Mo's mother vigorously. 'Mo tells me her share would be over eighty thousand pounds, and you may be right that she could get even more by keeping the business, but I think it's too much to gamble with. Your uncle recommends that we take the offer and I agree.'

'So, with the greatest respect' – it was Ned's father speaking again – 'I would like to propose that the partnership accept the offer of £250,000 from Gainsborough.'

'I will second that proposal,' said Mo's mother.

Felix said nothing. *We think you should take it . . .* That's what Ned's father had said, and it was only when he heard those words that he realized what was happening.

*We think . . .* meant that they had talked this over

beforehand. They had talked it over and made their decision before the meeting even started. Now they were going to vote on it and, under the terms of the partnership, all the partners had the same share of the voting power as they had of the money. Felix's share, at 42.5%, was the largest, but if the other three all voted against him, they would have the majority. And there was something else. Under the terms of the agreement, the final say on all matters of money was taken by the adults, not their children. If the three adults voted to sell, there was nothing, absolutely nothing, he could do to stop them.

'Felix?' Ned's father was looking at him. 'Are we going to vote on my proposal?'

'You're going to sit there and let this happen, are you?' Felix looked round the table at Mo and Ned and Ellie-Mae. 'You're just going to let them sell up?'

For Felix, what happened next was the worst part of it all. Mo did not look at him. Nor did the others. They looked at the table. They looked at their hands. They did not meet his gaze.

. . . And the truth hit him like a punch in the stomach.

*They already knew!* His friends had been sitting there for the last half hour, knowing what was going to happen, and none of them had said a word.

'I don't believe it!' Felix stared at them in horror. 'You knew?'

'We don't have any choice, Felix.' Mo was looking desperately unhappy as she spoke. 'They have the power and—'

'But . . . you're my friends!' said Felix. 'How could you *do* this?'

'A proposal has been put forward,' said Ned's uncle gently, 'and, with the greatest respect, I think it should be put to the vote.'

'We're only doing what we think is best,' said Mo's mother. 'And what your uncle advises.'

'All those in favour of accepting the proposed offer?' asked Ned's uncle, and he and Mo's mother and Ellie-Mae's grandmother raised their hands.

Felix's father had not raised his hand – he was clearly as surprised by what was happening as Felix – but it made no difference. A sudden burning anger welled up in Felix. How *dare* these people do this to him! They had no right! He stood up, pushing back his chair with enough force to knock it over.

'So that's it, is it?' He looked in turn at Mo, then Ned, then Ellie-Mae. 'You think this is OK, do you? To sit there and decide you'll take the money? Because it's not! This is *not* your business. It never was. It's *mine*! I thought of it.

It was my idea. I ran it. You think *any* of this would have happened without me? And you sit there now and you think you can just sell it away? Never mind what I think? Well, maybe you can, but this . . . this is all *wrong*. *Very* wrong. And you *know* it's wrong.'

'Please, Felix.' It was Mo, looking white-faced and upset. 'If you'd just listen—'

'No!' said Felix. 'I'm not going to listen. I'm not going to listen to any of you. In fact, I don't even want to be in the same room as any of you. Because I don't want to be anywhere near any of you. Ever again.'

And with that he walked out.


William came home from work in time to see his brother storming up the stairs.

'Has something happened?' he asked, putting a selection of glazed doughnuts on the table in the kitchen.

'As far as I can gather,' said his mother, 'they've just voted to sell your brother's business for £250,000.'

'Really?' William frowned. 'If I'd just sold a business for that much money, I think I'd look a lot more cheerful than he did.'

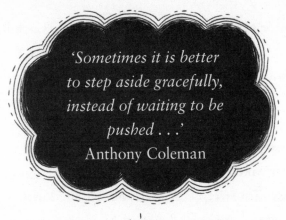

> *'Sometimes it is better
> to step aside gracefully,
> instead of waiting to be
> pushed . . .'*
> Anthony Coleman

CHAPTER TWENTY FIVE

# Close of Business

Three hours later Felix was lying on his bed, staring miserably at the ceiling, when his father appeared with the news that his uncle was downstairs.

He found Uncle Rufus standing in front of the fire-place in the front room. He hadn't shaved, his suit was wrinkled, and he looked badly in need of sleep.

'Your parents told me what happened,' he said, 'and I'm not surprised you're upset. I'm so sorry. It's all my fault.'

'It wasn't you,' said Felix. 'It was my so-called friends. They just sat there and let it happen! I still can't believe it.'

'It didn't sound like they had much choice.' Uncle Rufus ran his fingers through his hair. 'Your mother tells me the adults had already decided before the meeting started, and I can't say I blame them.' He sighed. 'They weren't supposed to know about the offer, you see. Not until you'd seen it and agreed it was OK.'

'They weren't supposed to know?'

Uncle Rufus crossed the room to sit down on the sofa, and gestured to Felix to sit beside him. 'What was *supposed* to happen was that I came round on Wednesday, as we arranged, told you about the offer and all the reasons why I thought you should take it, and then if you agreed – *if* you agreed – I had copies of the offer all printed up so you could give them to the others to pass on to their parents. Unfortunately, I wasn't here on Wednesday and my lovely wife only knew there was a letter on my desk that she thought you needed to see . . .' Uncle Rufus took off his glasses and rubbed his eyes. 'It's been a pretty disastrous week one way and another.'

'You thought I'd agree to selling Kardmart?'

'Yes, I did. It's a good offer.'

'But I don't want to sell! I like running Kardmart, and it's making a lot of money!'

'I didn't think you'd *want* to accept the offer,' said

Uncle Rufus, 'but I thought you'd *agree* to it when you saw the alternative.'

'What alternative?'

'I know you're still making money at the moment, but I don't think it's going to last. I'd say that in two or three years' time you'll be lucky if you're earning more than a few hundred a month. Certainly not a few thousand.'

Felix stared at his uncle. 'Why . . . why would you say that?'

'You asked me to find out why your sales have been falling,' said Uncle Rufus, 'and it turns out the reason is pretty simple. When you started Kardmart, hardly anybody had thought of selling cards on the internet. But they have now. Do you know how many companies set up websites selling greeting cards in this country in the last two months?'

Felix admitted that he didn't.

'Seventeen,' said Uncle Rufus. 'That's in the last two months. In this country. There are well over a hundred websites in the UK now selling cards. You got in early, before almost everyone else, but a lot of people have caught up with you now. And some are selling them even cheaper than you do. There's a dozen sites out there will sell you cards for fifty or sixty pence each. There's one website that will have the name of the person the card is for specially printed at the top. The big boys are moving in, backed by some big money, and you' – he pointed a finger at Felix – 'are being squeezed by the competition.'

Felix remembered something that his uncle had told him in one of their conversations about business. 'Can't we just do whatever they're doing, and do it better?'

'Well, you could, if you were prepared to spend thousands of pounds on advertising, set up a permanent office, pay a permanent staff. And of course it would help if you didn't have to spend most of the day at school. As it is, I can't see any way you can compete with the big hitters. And if you carry on the way you are . . . well, you'll probably still keep a steady core of buyers, but it'll mean selling a few cards less each month. I don't think it'll ever be like it was.'

Felix stared at him. There was something about the calm detached way that his uncle spoke that was horribly convincing.

'And that's why I thought, in the circumstances, that it might be worth exploring the idea of selling,' Uncle Rufus continued. 'So I got a friend of a friend to introduce me to the man at Gainsborough, and it turned out he was pretty keen to buy.

'They're an old-fashioned company, and it's suddenly dawned on them that they're getting left behind. They need to catch up with internet selling, and one of the quickest ways of doing that is to buy a small company that's already in the game. They like your cards – which they know are good and sell well – but what they like even more is your list of email addresses. All those thousands of people who already buy cards online that they can go back to and sell more cards to. That's what makes them keen to buy.

'They're offering a lot, and I thought you should take it. If you were deeply in love with the card business – if making cards was something you'd always cared passionately about – then I'd suggest you carried on with Kardmart. But that's not the case, is it? You set up the business because you thought it would make some money. That's all. And you were right, it did. But as your business adviser, I'm telling you it's time to move on from this one.'

Felix did not answer.

Uncle Rufus stood up. 'Anyway, that's what I was going to say to you on Wednesday if I hadn't been stuck in a hotel in Poland. So have a think about it, will you? If you still want to keep Kardmart, you can tell me tomorrow and we'll cancel the deal.'

'It's too late for that,' said Felix. 'The others have already agreed.'

'I'm your business adviser, not theirs,' said Uncle Rufus firmly. 'Nothing's been signed yet. It was only an offer, and offers can be withdrawn very easily. It's up to you.' He put a hand on Felix's shoulder. 'Your dad tells me Ludmila's invited you all to lunch tomorrow. Let's have another talk then, and you can tell me what you've decided. But I'm afraid, for now, I need to go home and get some sleep.'

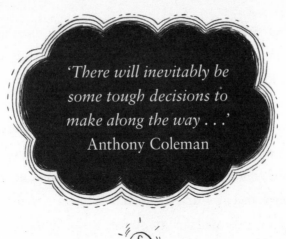

'There will inevitably be some tough decisions to make along the way . . .'
Anthony Coleman

CHAPTER TWENTY SIX

# Taking the Deal

Felix thought about it all that evening, and in bed that night, and the following morning he was still thinking about it. But a part of him knew that, in fact, he had already made the decision. It wasn't that difficult. It just wasn't one that he liked very much.

When his father drove them all out to his uncle's house for lunch, Uncle Rufus greeted them at the door looking a lot better than he had the day before. He led them all straight through to the kitchen and then out onto the terrace with the wicker chairs, where Ludmila was busy mixing a jug of something to drink that she said was very

191

popular in Slovakia. Uncle Rufus took a large glass for himself, gave a smaller one to Felix and said they would be back shortly, but that the two of them needed to have a word in private first.

He took Felix along the path that ran beside the back of the house and then in through some glass doors to the room that he used as an office. There were a couple of leather armchairs that faced out through the doorway, down towards the lake, and Uncle Rufus motioned Felix to one of them, and sat himself in the other.

'So,' he said, 'have you decided?'

Felix nodded. 'I'm going to take the offer. And I forgot to say thank you yesterday. For setting it up and everything.'

His uncle gave a dismissive wave of his hand. 'I'm only sorry it wasn't the solution you were hoping for.' He smiled sympathetically at his nephew. 'I know it isn't easy, but I think you've made the right decision. And you'll have ideas for other businesses, I promise you. Plenty of other ideas, I'm quite sure of that. And next time you'll find it much easier to get one off the ground because you'll have capital behind you. The first hundred thousand is always the hardest to make and you've already done it.'

'Next time, I'm going to make sure I own all the business myself,' said Felix. 'No partners. And no parents to interfere.'

'You don't want to be too hard on the parents,' said Uncle Rufus. 'They were only doing what they thought was best. Ned's dad wants to make sure that Ned can pay his way through university. Ellie-Mae's grandmother has all those cello lessons in London to pay for. Mo's mother thinks that having her daughter's cards printed by a major card company will help her get established in the art world – and she's right. They all are. Your friends have—'

'They're not my friends any more,' Felix interrupted determinedly. 'They *knew*. They knew what was being planned and they didn't tell me. That's not what friends do.'

'Ah . . . I see . . .' Uncle Rufus took a sip of his drink. 'Your mother told me you'd decided never to speak them again. Is that right? Did you mean it?'

'You bet I meant it,' said Felix. Mo had called round the night before and again that morning, but on both occasions he had refused to see her. 'Why should I talk to any of them? They betrayed me.'

'And that hurts?

'Yes. Yes, it hurts.'

'Of course it does . . .' Uncle Rufus sat for a moment, looking out at the garden. 'You know that woman I went to see? To sort things out with Ludmila? Dr Jameson. If she was here now, she'd tell you that it's not what your friends *did* that's hurting you, it's the story you're telling yourself about what they did.'

'I'm not telling myself any story. It's what happened.'

'Perhaps.'

'Not perhaps. It's the truth!'

'It's a *part* of the truth,' said Uncle Rufus, 'but not all of it, I think. And if Dr Jameson was here, she'd tell you there were other stories you could tell yourself that would still be true but which wouldn't hurt like that one does.'

'Other stories? Like what?'

'Well, I suppose one of them would go something like . . . Once upon a time, a boy called Felix Farmer had the idea of setting up a business selling cards. He had this friend who did these wonderful drawings and another friend who could build a website and another who could do the accounts, and they'd all known each other for years and the four of them set up in partnership together and were amazingly successful. They made thousands of pounds, but then the other three wanted to call it a day. Felix would have liked to carry on, but the others didn't want to – or at least their parents didn't – and so the business was sold.

'Now, that story is true as well. It's not *all* of the truth – any more than the one you've been telling yourself – but if I was in your place, I'd choose this second story, because at the end of it, you'd still have your friends. Who I've always rather liked by the way.

'You see, if you choose this second story, in years to come, whenever the four of you get together, you'll look back on what happened and you'll smile and you'll say, "Do you remember how at the start we wondered if we'd ever sell two hundred cards?" and, "Do you remember the first partnership meeting with all the ten-pound notes in the shoebox on the table?" And you'll think back and you'll all smile and laugh about it and remember what an extraordinary adventure it all was!'

Ludmila put her head round the door to say that lunch would be ready in five minutes, and Uncle Rufus gave her a nod and a wave before turning back to Felix.

'It's your choice, of course. Which story you choose to tell yourself is always your choice. But I learned from Dr Jameson that the smart thing, if you can do it, is to tell yourself the story that gives you the best ending.'

Felix did not answer. He was still very angry at the thought of what had happened, and the bitter taste of betrayal was still in his mouth, but . . . there was something else as well.

As his uncle had been speaking, the picture had flashed into his mind of the time, right at the start, when he had

195

called round to ask Mo if she had a card that might do for his mother's birthday and how she had answered the door, wrapped in a duvet and with a temperature of 39 degrees, and she hadn't told him to go away, but simply turned, led him indoors, found the disk for him and told him to print whatever he wanted.

And he remembered going to Ned, in the middle of a play rehearsal, and asking him to find out about websites, and how Ned had come right back the next day with the information he needed, and then agreed to build the website as well.

And Ellie-Mae had been in the middle of practising for a recital when he'd walked into the music room and told her he needed someone to sort out the accounts. And she'd come home with him after school the same day, like he had always known she would. He had always known that all of them would help, because they were . . . they were his friends.

And then there came into his mind a picture of what life would be like if they *weren't* his friends any more. If he went into school the next day and never spoke to any of them. It was a shock to realize how painful that would be – and yet that was what he had said he wanted. Never to talk to any of them again.

And was his uncle right when he said he thought it

sounded like they hadn't had much choice? Was it really fair to say that what they had done was so wrong? The picture came to his mind of Mo's white face at the table . . . Of Mo calling round the night before and again that morning . . .

'I told myself a story once.' Uncle Rufus was staring out through the glass doors towards the lake. 'About how I had been betrayed. I told it to myself for twenty years and I so wish now that I hadn't. It was a story that meant I missed out on being with some very good people.'

He was silent for several seconds, before standing up and turning to Felix.

'Let's go and have some lunch, shall we?' he said.

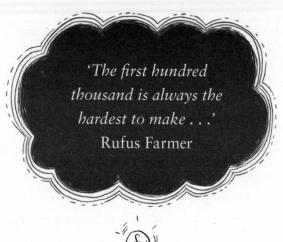

'The first hundred
thousand is always the
hardest to make . . .'
Rufus Farmer

CHAPTER TWENTY SEVEN

# Capital Gains

'I might,' said Felix, as they were driving home after the
lunch with Uncle Rufus, 'go and see Mo when we get
back.'

'Sounds like an excellent idea,' said his mother from
the front passenger seat.

'I thought you said you were never going to talk to her
again.' William was sitting beside Felix in the back.

'I know. But I've been thinking that maybe . . . maybe
she was only doing what she thought was best.'

'Good for you,' said Mr Farmer. 'A very mature
attitude.'

'So you're going to apologize or something?' asked William.

'No, of course I'm not,' said Felix. 'Why would I apologize?'

'So what *are* you going to say?'

Felix had not entirely sorted that bit out yet. Until the moment he announced it, he had not even decided that he would go and see Mo. Now, however, he wondered what he *was* going to say when he called round, and was suddenly not sure if it was a good idea after all. He wanted things to be back the way they were, but getting there after everything that had happened might not be as simple as he had thought.

'He doesn't have to say anything,' said Mrs Farmer. 'He can use the code.'

'The code?'

Felix's mother swivelled round in the passenger seat. 'The code is when you tell people something, but without actually saying it out loud,' she explained. 'It can save a lot of embarrassment.'

Felix frowned.

'If you want to make up with Mo, for example,' his mother continued, 'you go round to her house and say you've come to . . . return a pen she left behind at the meeting yesterday.'

'That's code for you're not angry any more,' Mr Farmer put in from the driver's seat.

'Will she know that?'

'Oh yes.' Mrs Farmer smiled. 'Mo knows all about the code. Of course, she doesn't know *you* know about it, so she'll want to check she's not making a mistake, and she'll say something like, "Do you want to come in for a bit?"'

'Which is code for "I'm glad you're not angry, yes, I'd like to make up as well,"' said Mr Farmer.

'So you say thank you and you go in, you chat for a bit, and then at some point she'll say something like, "Look, about yesterday . . ." And that's when *you* say, "Hey, nothing to worry about. You did what you thought was best . . ." And then she gives you a hug, which is girl code for, "What a relief, I thought you were never going to talk to me again." And there you are, it's done.'

'Are you *sure* about all this?' asked William.

'Quite sure,' said Felix's mother firmly.

Mr Farmer peered briefly at Felix in the rear-view mirror and smiled. 'It won't be exactly like that, of course, but something close.'

'And by the time you get to school tomorrow,' said Mrs Farmer, 'Mo will already have told the others, and by lunchtime you'll all be back together as friends.'

Felix wondered if it could possibly be quite that easy.

He was not entirely convinced, but then he remembered something. How, on the first day his father had driven him over to see Uncle Rufus, he had come out of the house at the end of the meeting to find both his parents waiting outside. His mother, he remembered, had walked straight over and given Uncle Rufus a hug. It was months later that he discovered that the two of them had not spoken for twenty years, but his mother hadn't said a word. Simply walked over and hugged him.

So perhaps she was right, and you didn't always have to use words to say something . . .

Felix walked round to Mo's house soon after they got home.

'Hi,' he said, when she answered the door. 'You left this at our house yesterday.' He held out a pen.

'Did I? Oh . . . thanks.' Mo took the pen and, after a moment's hesitation, added, 'Do you want to come in for a bit?'

'Yes, all right.' Felix followed her indoors, and then up the stairs as she led the way into her new art room. She closed the door behind them, and stood there, looking at him.

'So what are you working on?' asked Felix, gesturing at the drawing board under the window. 'Anything interesting?'

'Only school work at the moment.' Mo looked for a moment as if she were going to show him the drawing, but then changed her mind.

'Look,' she said, 'about yesterday . . .'

'It's OK,' said Felix. 'Nothing to worry about. You did what you thought was best.'

'No, I didn't,' said Mo. 'It was Mum. She insisted. I could have killed her . . .'

'I'm sure she was only doing what she thought was best,' said Felix. 'And we've had a good run, haven't we? Made a lot of money and it's . . . it's all been quite an adventure, hasn't it!'

'Yes,' said Mo. 'Yes, it has and . . . Look, are you *sure* it's all right?'

'Quite sure,' said Felix.

'Oh, that is *such* a relief!' Mo took a breath and blew it out again. 'You frightened the life out of me, you know! I really thought you were never going to talk to me again!'

She took two steps towards him. It looked for a moment as if she was about to hug him, but instead she thumped him on the arm. Quite hard.

'Please! Don't *ever* do anything like that again,' she said.

And then she hugged him.

*

It all worked out very satisfactorily at school the next day as well. As his mother had said, word had clearly been passed to the others, and Ellie-Mae greeted him at the school gates with a hug even tighter than Mo's had been and pushed a letter into his hand that said how grateful she was for all he had done, how sorry she was for what had happened, and how she hoped more than anything that they could still be friends.

Ned didn't actually hug Felix, but he explained, on at least four separate occasions through the day, how his father had only told him on the Saturday morning about his plan to vote in favour of accepting the offer, and how he hadn't realized that Mo's mother and Ellie-Mae's gran would be doing the same, and how he wished he'd said something, and was Felix *really* all right about it?

Felix told him, on each occasion, that yes, he was all right, and the curious thing was that, when he said it, he really *was* all right. Somehow, and Felix never knew exactly how it happened, the anger and the bitterness seemed to have evaporated as unexpectedly as they had first appeared, and he was left with his friends again.

And – as his father pointed out – quite a lot of money.

He had already started wondering what he might do with it.

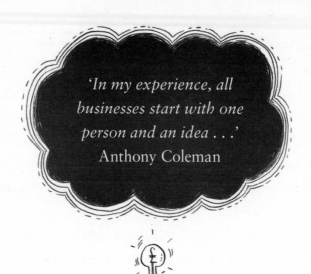

CHAPTER TWENTY EIGHT

# Start Up

Uncle Rufus organized a party to celebrate selling Kardmart to Gainsborough. The actual signing over of the assets happened up in Birmingham in the last week of September, but he said he thought there ought to be some event to mark the official ending of the partnership, and invited Ned, Mo, Ellie-Mae and their families out to his house the following Saturday for one last partnership meeting. The party turned out to be quite a lavish affair.

As well as the four partners, Uncle Rufus had invited anyone who had played any part in the Kardmart story. So Felix's grandmother was there, as the person who had kick-started the whole thing by asking Felix to print some copies for her of the card he had given his mother. Mr Minchin, the owner of WePrintAnything, was there, describing to anyone who would listen, how surprised he had been to find the customers placing an order worth several thousands of pounds had turned out to be a group of thirteen-year-olds. Alan, the man who had fixed Felix's computer without charging him had also been invited, as had Mr Hughes, the sixth form teacher who had asked Felix to come and talk to his students. He took the opportunity to ask Felix to do the same for his latest batch of students, but Felix told him that Ned, with his business building websites, might be a more relevant speaker now that he no longer had a business himself.

The one person Uncle Rufus had invited who was not, sadly, able to join them, was Anthony Coleman, the author of *Everything You Need to Know About Setting Up Your Own Business*. He lived in France these days, but sent a card with his congratulations and good wishes for success in the future. It said he could not have been more pleased to hear that his little book had been of some assistance to a new generation of entrepreneurs.

Perhaps best of all, however, Uncle Rufus had some-how managed to get hold of a good many of the original class of 5FW – all the characters who had featured in the cards that Mo had drawn. Mr Minchin had printed off huge blown-up copies of the drawings, which Ludmila had hung all around the house, and you could see people standing in front of them and recognizing themselves and each other. Samar was there, more beautiful than ever, and still surrounded by boys. Barry was there, with a pair of rats in his coat pocket, and the accident-prone Dylan, to everyone's delight, turned up with his head in a bandage having been hit on the head that afternoon by a cricket ball.

Even old Mr Wilkins, who had taken them on Nature Walks, was there, and could be seen soon after the party started, sleeping contentedly in an armchair in the hall.

Once everyone had arrived, they were ushered into the dining room for the four partners to sign the papers that would officially bring the partnership to a close, and Uncle Rufus gave a little speech outlining the story of the enterprise for those who did not know its details.

The partnership had, he said, sold an astonishing 134,180 cards in eighteen months, before selling their business for a quarter of a million pounds. And he went on to tell the story of how Felix had had the original idea, how he had brought in his friends to help, and about the day he had astonished his parents with the shoebox full of ten-pound notes. He described how he had first become involved himself, and the pleasure it had given him to watch the growing success of four such talented young businessmen and women in the months that followed.

Uncle Rufus, Felix knew, was very good at making a group of people feel pleased with themselves. It was almost the first thing he had done at the first partnership meeting, and he often said that one of the jobs of a business manager was to remind people if they were doing something well. As his uncle was speaking, Felix looked round the room at the beaming faces and the smiles of his friends, and felt a little shiver at the thought of how close he had come to telling himself a story that would have had a very different ending. An ending that would not have had any of the warmth and celebration of this one, but that would have left him feeling as he had that other Saturday – angry, friendless, resentful and alone.

Of all the many things he had to thank his uncle for, he thought that particular piece of advice, to tell himself a different story, was probably the one for which he would always be the most grateful.

Uncle Rufus found him, half an hour later, in the kitchen.

'You said you wanted to talk to me about something?' he asked.

'Well, if you had time,' Felix said.

'Let's go and find somewhere quiet, shall we?' Uncle Rufus looked around the room. 'It's a bit noisy in here.'

He led the way across the kitchen to a door on the far side and, following his uncle, Felix found that it led straight through into the garage.

Like everything else about his uncle's house, the garage was big. It had four double doors on the right that led out onto the drive and, as well as his uncle's silver Lexus, it contained a Range Rover, a Toyota truck and—

Felix stopped in his tracks. Directly in front of him was a low, sleek, open-topped red sports car and he didn't need to see the badge on the bonnet with the black horse on a yellow background to know what it was.

'I don't believe it!' he said. 'You've bought a Ferrari!'

'Delivered yesterday,' said his uncle with a smile.

'I used to dream of having one of these . . .' Felix reached out a hand and stroked his fingers along the side.

'Yes,' said his uncle. 'I remember.'

'Was it very expensive?'

'Forty thousand. There's a man I do business with sometimes, needed some ready cash quickly, and it was too good an offer to refuse.'

Forty thousand pounds was a lot of money, but it was, Felix knew, something of a bargain for a Ferrari F355.

'You want to sit in it?'

His uncle had pulled open the door to the driver's seat and Felix climbed in. The seats were covered in soft black leather, as was the steering wheel. Uncle Rufus went round the other side and got in the passenger seat.

'I cannot believe you own a Ferrari!'

'Well . . .' said Uncle Rufus. 'Strictly speaking, I don't.'

'But I thought you said—'

'I bought this car,' said Uncle Rufus, 'with some of the money you asked me to invest. I'd been wondering where would be the best place to put it, and the classic car market seems pretty strong at the moment, so I thought . . . why not?'

'You bought this car with my money?'

'It's a slightly unusual investment, but I don't think you'll regret it.' Uncle Rufus gestured at the dashboard. 'It appeared, briefly, in a James Bond movie – I forget which one – but that gives a nudge to its value. I'm pretty sure, if you wanted to sell it, that I could get at least fifty, possibly fifty-five. If you don't fancy the risk, I'll be happy to buy it off you myself, but if you do decide to keep it, you're very welcome to leave it here.'

It took a while for his uncle's meaning to sink in.

'You mean . . . this is *my* Ferrari?'

'It is. Though you can't drive it on the road yet, I'm afraid. Not for a few years anyway.'

Felix was hardly listening. This was *his* Ferrari. He *owned* it!

'Try turning the key,' said his uncle.

The key was in the ignition and when Felix turned it there was an instant response. He put his foot gently on the accelerator and a wonderful throaty roar filled the garage.

Eventually, he turned off the engine and sat there in contented silence.

'It's only a bit of fun, of course,' his uncle said. 'You may not want to keep it, but I don't think you'll lose on it, whatever you decide.' He leaned back in his seat. 'Anyway, what was it you wanted to talk about?'

'Well,' said Felix, 'I was going to ask your advice.'

'Let me guess. You've got an idea for a new business.'

'Yes. Yes, I have.'

Uncle Rufus smiled. 'I thought you might!'


'Have you seen Felix anywhere?' asked Mr Farmer, peering round the throng of people in the kitchen.

'Last I saw, he was heading out through there.' Mo pointed to the door on the far side of the kitchen.

'Did he look all right?' asked Mrs Farmer.

'I think so. Why?'

'We're a bit worried about him,' said Felix's father.

'He's gone sort of quiet and thoughtful recently. We wondered if he was still upset about having to sell the business.'

'Could you put a head round the door and check he's OK?' said Felix's mother. 'Only I wouldn't like to think he was sitting somewhere all miserable on his own.'

'My brother works at this bakery,' said Felix, 'and the man who owns it has had some heart trouble, and wants to sell.'

'Oh, yes?'

'I went round there with Ellie-Mae to talk to him, and the thing is the business is making good money. I've got the figures here . . .' Felix reached into a pocket and took out a piece of paper. 'I think if I bought the shop, then rented it to my brother – him and his girlfriend have got all sorts of ideas for growing the place – I should get quite a good return. What do you think?'

Uncle Rufus took the sheet of paper, and studied it. 'Interesting,' he said, with a gleam in his eye. 'Definitely interesting . . .'

They were both so engrossed in discussing the possibility that neither of them noticed Mo put her head round the door from the kitchen, listen for a while, then quietly go back out, closing the door behind her.

*

'Well?' asked Mrs Farmer.

'He's fine,' said Mo.

'You're sure? He doesn't look upset or anything?'

'He's with his uncle,' said Mo, 'and he looks very happy. In fact . . . I'm not sure I've ever seen him so happy.'

'Really?' Mr Farmer looked at her. 'Why? What's he doing?'

'He's sitting in a Ferrari,' said Mo, 'talking business.'